In the distance she could finally hear the sirens and prayed they arrived before the flames reached the barn.

"Isabelle? You okay?"

Mac's voice came from the other end of the building. "I'm okay. One more horse then we can get out of here."

"I've got him," he said. Through the thickening smoke, she saw him heading for the last stall. She tried to draw in a breath and got a lungful of smoke that sent her into a coughing fit.

"Get out, Isabelle!"

She had no choice. She couldn't breathe. But she couldn't leave Mac. "Just hurry," she pleaded. She dropped to the dirt floor and found the air still smoky, but better. She managed to grab a lungful, then shot to her feet. "Mac?"

"Go!"

"Where are you?" She let out another cough, feeling like she was suffocating. Flames flickered from the other end of the barn and terror seized her. "Mac! We have to go now!"

Lynette Eason is a bestselling, award-winning author who makes her home in South Carolina with her husband and two teenage children. She enjoys traveling, spending time with her family and teaching at various writing conferences around the country. She is a member of Romance Writers of America and American Christian Fiction Writers. Lynette can often be found online interacting with her readers. You can find her on Facebook.com/lynette.eason and on Twitter, @lynetteeason.

Books by Lynette Eason

Love Inspired Suspense

Holiday Homecoming Secrets
Peril on the Ranch

True Blue K-9 Unit

Justice Mission

Wrangler's Corner

The Lawman Returns
Rodeo Rescuer
Protecting Her Daughter
Classified Christmas Mission
Christmas Ranch Rescue
Vanished in the Night
Holiday Amnesia

Military K-9 Unit

Explosive Force

Classified K-9 Unit

Bounty Hunter

Visit the Author Profile page at Harlequin.com for more titles.

PERIL ON THE RANCH

LYNETTE EASON

LOVE INSPIRED SUSPENSE
INSPIRATIONAL ROMANCE

LOVE INSPIRED®SUSPENSE

INSPIRATIONAL ROMANCE

ISBN-13: 978-1-335-72246-1

Recycling programs
for this product may
not exist in your area.

Peril on the Ranch

Love Inspired
22 Adelaide St. West, 40th Floor
Toronto, Ontario M5H 4E3, Canada
www.Harlequin.com

Printed in U.S.A.

For I know the thoughts that I think toward you, saith the Lord, thoughts of peace, and not of evil, to give you an expected end.
—*Jeremiah* 29:11

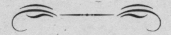

Dedicated to my family. I love you more than words can express. Thank you for all the love and support a writer, mom and wife could ask for.

ONE

Isabelle Trent woke with a start. She lay still, trying to figure out what had jarred her just as the sun was beginning to make its way above the horizon. She'd forgotten to pull her curtains closed before she'd fallen into bed with a half-finished prayer on her lips.

Maybe it was just the light that had disturbed her.

A faint cry reached her.

Or maybe not. One of the children?

Isabelle threw off the covers and hurried to pull on her robe and slippers. She darted out of the bedroom and into the hall, pausing to listen. Nothing. She went to the room nearest hers and peered in. The twin beds on opposite walls each held one child. Twelve-year-old Danny Billings and fourteen-year-old Zeb Hammrick, who'd become best of friends since being placed with her. Zeb had arrived first, two months ago. Danny had come a short two days later. Both boys slept the deep sleep of those without worries—exactly what she'd worked so hard to help them do.

In the next room, five-year-old Katie Miller snored gently, her left arm wrapped around the neck of the little doll she was never without.

The sound reached Isabelle's ears once more coming from farther away. A cry that sounded like…a baby? A kitten? She retraced her steps back to her bedroom, bypassed it and stepped into the great room.

The sound grew louder, and it came from the wraparound porch just ahead.

Finally, she identified it.

A baby.

With a soft gasp, Isabelle hurried forward to unlock the French door and step outside. A brisk October wind whipped her hair around her face and chills skated up her spine. The wood creaked beneath her weight and the crying stopped for a brief second before resuming at an ear-piercing decibel level. She flipped the light on.

At her feet, an infant was strapped into a carrier. A heavy wool blanket covered the baby. A small box sat next to the carrier. "Oh, my sweet little one." Isabelle released the straps and scooped the tiny body, blanket and all, into her arms. Sniffles and hiccups greeted her. A piece of paper fluttered from the blanket back into the carrier as the baby jammed a fist into its mouth.

Another angry wail rattled the roof. "Okay, I hear you. You're definitely hungry." She knelt to check the box and breathed a sigh of relief when she found a full bottle and a can of formula, along with a pack of diapers and wipes. She snatched the bottle and shook it. How long had it been in there? It was room temperature, so it was probably fine. If it had been out much longer, it would have been cold thanks to the temperatures hovering in the midforty range.

Movement from the edge of the porch caught her attention. "Hey, who's there?" She stuck the nipple into the baby's mouth, and blessed quiet ensued.

The figure moved, slipping away from the glow of the light.

The slow-moving sun only revealed the silhouette of the person simply standing there. Not moving. Just watching. Male or female, she couldn't tell. Unease crawled through her. "Hey, is this your baby?"

Again, nothing. But she thought it might be a man. Then again, the lanky form could be an older teen. His hoodie-covered head swiveled left, then right. She tried to see his face hidden by the cloth but could only make out a shadow. "Hello?"

Still, he stayed silent. He looked back over his shoulder one more time, then seemed to make up his mind about something. Her nerves jangled and alarm shuddered through her. He took a step toward her and Isabelle spun. Holding the infant in the crook of her left arm, she twisted the knob with her right hand and pushed the door open just wide enough for her to slip through. She shut the door and locked it.

Her phone sat on her nightstand in her bedroom, but she was too busy worrying about if she'd locked the other doors. Heart pounding, she watched the figure through the glass while the baby was content to suck down the contents of the bottle.

He moved as though to leave, then turned back, dark eyes on hers. He came toward the glass door, reaching for the knob. Clutching the baby, Isabelle whirled and raced to her bedroom to snatch her phone from the nightstand. She dialed 911 and hurried back to the den area to see the dark-clad figure pacing in front of her door. Quick as lightning, he spun and slammed a fist on the wooden part of the door. The noise jarred the infant, who let out a wail.

"911. What's your emergency?"

"Someone's trying to get in my house." Breathless, she rattled off her address over the baby's cries. She pushed the bottle back into the child's mouth and the wails ceased. "He's outside on the porch and I'm afraid he's going to break the glass and push his way in."

"Can you get somewhere safe?"

"No, I can't leave the house. I'm a foster mother and I have four children here." She hurried to the garage door and twisted the dead bolt. The lower knob was locked.

"Other adults?"

"One in the apartment above the garage, but she's sixty-five years old. I don't want her down here. One man, who's also in his sixties, in the bunkhouse." Her parents lived on the same land, through the trees and up the hill about half a mile away, but she wasn't about to call them.

She lost sight of the intruder as he rounded the corner of the porch. Isabelle hurried to keep him in her sights. As she stepped into the living area facing the front of the home, she spotted the headlights of a vehicle coming up the drive. A quick glance at the front door reassured her it was secure, with the dead bolt on and the chain in place.

The truck pulled to the top of her U-shaped drive and stopped. Who—? She spotted the time. 7:30. Brian McGee. Mac. The man she was supposed to interview this morning for the ranch foreman job. He was early, and she couldn't let him get out of the truck with a potentially dangerous person on the loose.

Isabelle unlatched the nearest window and raised it a fraction.

"Izzy-belle, what's going on?" Five-year-old Katie stood just inside the living area, rubbing the sleep from her eyes. "Why do I keep hearing a baby cry?"

"Hang on just a second, honey." She set the baby on the floor, keeping an eye on the driver of the decades-old truck. He was just sitting there, looking around. What was he doing? She turned to Katie. "Come sit with this little one for a minute, okay?"

Katie trotted over to plop down next to the child, who clutched the bottle with both hands. "She's cute."

All babies were *she* to Katie. Isabelle hadn't had a chance to find out if that was an accurate description, yet. Finally, the person she thought was there for the interview opened the truck door. "Get back in your truck," she called. "There's an intruder on the property!"

"A 'truder?" Katie looked up with a frown. "What's that?"

The man stilled. "Where is he?"

"He went around the side of the house. The police are on the way, but he might be dangerous. Please, get back in your truck and lock the door." She wasn't about to urge him inside her home until she knew exactly who he was. He could always drive away if he needed to.

The sound of breaking glass pulled a gasp from her. "I think he's trying to get in the kitchen!"

Mac bolted from the truck just as the sun crested the horizon and spread light around the area. He raced around the side of the house to the back and skidded to a stop. The intruder the owner had mentioned had one foot inside the window and his gloved hands gripped the molding. Mac darted forward, placed his hands on the porch railing and vaulted over it. He landed on the wooden flooring with a thud and faced the frozen figure now half in and half out of the house. "Don't do it, man," Mac said. "Cops are on the way."

His words seemed to send indecision sweeping through the guy. A pause Mac took advantage of. He lunged, grabbed two fistfuls of the hoodie material and pulled him away from the window. A heavy fist glanced off Mac's cheek. He winced and jerked back, losing his grip. That gave the wiry figure the opening he needed, and he darted away from Mac to dash down the length of the porch, leap over the steps and head full-speed across the pasture. Mac pounded after him.

The guy broke through the tree line and disappeared into the woods. Mac did the same seconds later, only to stop when he realized he'd lost him. Mac turned, listening, his eyes searching. Finally, he heard the crunching of underbrush to his left and headed that way, hit a patch of mud and slid almost falling. He managed to catch his balance, but a second later, the roar of a motorcycle captured his attention. After one last push through tree limbs and vines, he found himself staring at the back of a disappearing bike. He didn't know where the trail led, but there was no way he'd catch the guy on foot. With a sigh, he gave up the chase and retraced his steps.

When he came to the pasture beyond the tree line, he could see the woman who was, hopefully, his future boss. Isabelle Trent. She stood on the front porch, a little girl about five years old clutching Isabelle's knee with one hand and a doll with her other. Isabelle cradled an infant in the crook of her right arm.

Dressed in jeans, boots and a long-sleeved red flannel shirt, she had her blond hair pulled into a messy ponytail. It struck him that she looked comfortable and completely in her element. If understandably shaken.

Two police officers faced her. One wrote notes in a little black book while the other spoke into the radio on her shoulder. As Mac approached, Isabelle's green eyes landed on him, and the officers turned. Mac made sure they could see his hands.

"That's the man who came to the rescue," Isabelle said.

Mac relaxed a fraction. "Sorry, I couldn't catch him. He had a motorcycle stashed in the woods and got to it before I could get to him." He climbed the steps and stood beside her, facing the officers. "I'm Brian McGee but call me Mac."

"I'm Isabelle Trent. I've already told them who you are. I'm glad to hear I guessed correctly." The baby in her arms yawned and closed bright blue eyes. The little girl watched him with wide gray eyes. Her dark ringlets tumbled over her shoulders and down to her waist. She had on pink pajamas and fuzzy pink slippers.

"You did."

"Well, welcome to Timber Creek and the Jo-Belle Ranch. I'm sure it was a unique introduction to the place."

"Yes, ma'am. Can't say I've ever had a welcome quite like that before. JoBelle?" He'd wondered about the name.

"My husband's name was Josiah. I'm Isabelle. JoBelle." She shrugged. "We liked it."

"Makes sense."

"These are Deputies Grant Hathaway and Regina Jacobson," Isabelle said. Mac shook hands with each of them. "They're good friends of mine. Regina and I went to high school together. Grant was a few years ahead of us."

"We just got here about two minutes ago," Grant said. "There was a tree across the back road that leads up here. We had to loop around and come in the main way. Glad to see you didn't run into trouble or need any assistance with that guy."

"I don't think he had a weapon on him, but I can't say for sure. He was quick, though. Ran like a jackrabbit."

"We'll need a description."

"I'll give what I can, but I'm not sure it'll help. He had a baseball cap and a hoodie on, so his face was fairly well hidden. He also had on ratty jeans and black gloves."

Grant took notes.

"He had a goatee," Isabelle said. "I saw that for a split second when he was trying to get in the French doors off the den. Then again, right before Mac pulled him out of the window, I got a flash of it."

"That's good information. Anything else?"

"Nothing that I can think of," Isabelle said.

Mac shrugged. "I'd agree with the goatee. The baseball hat under the hoodie was red and gold with a logo on it, but I didn't recognize it." He went back to the moment he'd pulled the guy from the window, the moment that had provided his best look at the man's features. "Sorry, that's all I've got for now. I didn't even see the motorcycle for long. Just caught a glimpse as he went around a curve on the trail."

Another car pulled into the driveway and Isabelle shifted the infant to her other shoulder. Katie stayed put, and Mac wondered at Isabelle's unfazed demeanor. A baby on her shoulder and one attached to her leg. It looked completely natural for her. His thoughts went to another child and pain shafted him.

He let her voice pull him from a past he didn't want to remember.

"That's Cheryl Younts," she said. "She's with Child Protection Services." Isabelle gently patted the baby on the back. "Someone dropped this little darling off on my front porch this morning. I think the guy you chased either dropped her off or was on his way to come get her when I beat him to it." She frowned. "I asked him if the baby was his, but he never said a word. He acted unsure at first. Then seemed to make up his mind and started coming toward us. He was…menacing. Scary. That's when I ran and locked us in the house and then called 911."

"I'm glad I got here early," Mac said.

"Trust me, I'm glad, too. I shudder to think what would have happened if you hadn't managed to pull him out of the window."

Ms. Younts stepped out of her vehicle and approached with a frown on her face. "Isabelle?"

"Thanks for coming so quickly."

"I didn't have much choice. You told me you needed me ASAP and to please hurry." She eyed the two officers. "What's going on?"

Mac wanted to hear the answer to that question, too.

"Follow me," Isabelle said.

They made their way back to the area near the front door and Isabelle pointed to the carrier. "I haven't had a chance to look at it yet, but I think there's a note in there."

Mac was the closest, so he leaned down and snagged the piece of paper. "It says, 'This is Lilly. She's eight months old and I can't take care of her anymore. I know you're a good mother to the kids that you have, so please be a good mom to Lilly. She's a sweet baby and loves to fall asleep to music or have you sing to her. Thank you. Please tell her that her mommy loves her.'" He looked up. "That's it."

"Lilly," Isabelle said. "A sweet name for this

little girl." She turned to Cheryl. "Are you all right with her staying with me?"

"Of course. You're all up-to-date on your emergency placement status, so that's a good thing. I'll have to take her to the doctor for a checkup, do some other paperwork, of course, to make it all official and legal, but that won't take me long. I can email it to you later this afternoon."

"Perfect. Now I just need to get the crib put together."

"I can do that," Mac said.

"I haven't interviewed you, yet," she reminded him.

"Oh. Right."

"Have you done a lot of ranch work?"

"Yes, ma'am. Granted, not a place as big as this one as I was working a full-time job as well, but I used to have my own small ranch before life happened. Now I'm something of a drifter, but I'm harmless."

"I know. Your background check came back clean."

"Well, that's good to know," Cheryl said. "I'll need a copy of that for the file."

Isabelle nodded to Cheryl, then turned back to him. "As long as you can do the work, you're hired."

Mac blinked. "Just like that?"

"Just like that. Now, that was the easy part."

"Isabelle?" The husky voice caught his attention and he noticed two boys standing in the doorway. "What's going on?" the taller one asked.

"Zeb, Danny," Isabelle said, "this is Mac. Mac, this is Zeb Hammrick and Danny Billings. Guys, we had a little excitement this morning. I'll fill you in later, but for now, Mac is going to be working around here."

"Cool," Zeb said. "Welcome to the ranch."

"Thanks."

Zeb looked up at Isabelle. "We're hungry. Is it okay if I make pancakes? Ms. Sybil already left for that doctor's appointment today, remember?"

"Of course. I'll be there in just a bit. And you might want to hurry a bit. The school bus will be here in about thirty minutes. Take Katie with you, will you?"

The kids disappeared back into the house and Isabelle bit her lip while the baby snoozed on her shoulder. "That was scary, y'all. These kids have suffered enough trauma in their lives. And while Katie seems to be unaffected and the boys didn't see any of it, they don't need this kind of thing."

The officers exchanged a glance. "What do you think he was after?"

"I have no idea. Probably money or something he could easily pawn." She glanced at the infant in her arms. "Or the baby, maybe? I don't know why."

Mac shoved his hands into his pockets and eyed the officers, then Isabelle. "Because it means he didn't get what he was after."

Isabelle nodded, the dread in her eyes letting him know she understood immediately where he was going with that statement. She drew in a deep breath and raked a hand over her ponytail. "And you think he might come back."

TWO

Isabelle shuddered at the thought that the intruder might return to finish whatever his objective had been. Had he thought no one was home when he approached in the early-morning hour? Or had he been watching and knew she was basically alone with the children in the house and thought he could take what he wanted without fear she'd fight back?

He would have been correct if it meant protecting the children. She swallowed at the visual her imagination produced. Okay, then. "What if he was the one who left the baby and then changed his mind?"

"That's not what the note indicates," Grant said. "Like you suggested, he was probably just looking for something to steal and you surprised him."

"But why didn't he just run when he realized I was here?"

Regina shrugged. "He might have been

strung out and desperate. We won't know until we catch him and ask him."

"Well, I hope that's soon." In the distance, she could see signs of life in the bunkhouse attached to the barn. Two dogs, Milo and Sugar, bounded out of the small living quarters and sprinted toward them. She pointed. "That man heading this way is Cody Ray," she said for Mac's benefit. "He runs the barn and takes care of the horses. We have a lot of people who board with us." Milo and Sugar barked and tumbled over each other, playing tag in the open space. "The black Lab is Milo and the border collie is Sugar. They belong to Cody Ray, but they're great with the kids."

Cody Ray reached them, a frown on his face and questions in his eyes, while the dogs approached with wagging tails. "What's going on out here?" he asked.

Isabelle made the introductions and brought him up to speed on the events of the morning. His ruddy face paled. "I didn't hear a thing. And the dogs didn't alert to anything wrong."

"You were too far away, Cody," Isabelle said. "The whole thing lasted less than five minutes."

"What about Sybil?"

"I had forgotten in the moment, but she was gone before the sun came up." Relief flickered in his eyes and Isabelle smiled. His soft spot for the widowed cook wasn't any secret. She turned to the officers. "If anything else comes up, I'll call, I guess."

Regina nodded. "I don't live too far from you, Iz. You know you can call me anytime."

"I know. Thanks, Regina."

"We're going to head out," Grant said. "Let us know if you think of anything else. We'll also make it a point to drive out here two or three times a day for the next few days."

Isabelle nodded. "That would be great, thanks."

After the officers drove away, Isabelle let out a long, slow breath. "All right, let me get the kids off to school and we'll sit down and talk about things."

"And I'll take the baby to the doctor," Cheryl said. "I'll bring her back as soon as we're finished."

Isabelle nodded. "I'll be ready for her."

Forty-five minutes later, Isabelle sat in her small office off the den. After Cheryl had left, she'd shown Mac his living space and he'd seemed pleased and grateful for the nice area. He'd be staying in the furnished mother-in-law suite attached to the main house with his own room, bathroom and den. The separate entrance meant he could come and go as he pleased without worrying about disturbing her or the children.

And now she had to go over her finances so

she could decide what to buy for the baby. Isabelle had a few toys for an infant Lilly's age, but she'd need diapers, more formula, some jars of baby food and, at the very least, a week's worth of clothing. Fortunately, there was a children's consignment store on Main Street and Isabelle planned to head there as soon as Mac had signed the employment papers.

A knock on the door pulled her attention from the computer screen. "Come in." Mac stepped inside and she waved to the nearest chair. "Please, have a seat."

"Thanks."

While he got settled, she studied him. He had dark curly hair that looked finger-combed, but she liked it. Dark eyes and olive skin made her wonder about his heritage. Whatever it was, he was a very handsome man and she found herself drawn to it.

Isabelle cleared her throat and slid the papers across the desk in front of him, then handed him a pen. "I'm the one who should be thanking you. Again."

He smiled and scribbled his signature across the bottom of the various forms. "Glad I was here." He pushed the documents back to her. "Just out of curiosity," he said, "how many people applied for this job?"

"Five. And I've canceled the three remaining interviews."

He blinked. "Why me?"

"You chased down a would-be burglar, and you look honest."

A huff of laughter escaped him. "You're hiring me because I look honest?"

"Well, that, and your background check came back squeaky clean. Your résumé said you're a former police officer?"

"Yes."

"And you wanted to get off that line of work because…?"

His green eyes stayed on her but went dark and he lifted a hand to rub his strong jaw. "It was time for a change."

She knew he was hiding something. But her gut said it was something personal, not something that would affect his job or something she needed to worry about safety-wise. At least she was mostly certain of that. However, he was entitled to his privacy, so she let it drop. "I can understand the need for change." She shifted her gaze to the papers in front of her. "Just one more question. Your résumé is rather short. How long were you at your last couple of jobs?"

He nodded. "After I left law enforcement I followed the rodeo circuit for a while. Did some bull riding and roping. I won some and lost some. I had a hard hit in the last one and figured I'd get out while I was still in one piece. From there, I worked with a construction crew for eight months while we built houses in a new neighborhood. Once that was done, I wanted to move on and decided to look for another job in this area. I saw your ad in the paper and…here I am. In Timber Creek, North Carolina."

"Yes," she said, her voice soft. "Here you are. How long do you think you'll stay?"

For a moment, he looked away and then studied his hands. Finally, he looked up. "You're right. I'm honest. I can't say how long I'll stick around, but I'll do my best work while I'm here and I'll give you a month's notice before I leave."

She bit her lip, wondering if she should tell him he wasn't the right man for the job after all, but…

Again, the feeling that he was running from something flitted through her mind. However, she also felt like she could trust him. "All right, then. Thanks for being straight with me." She snagged a paper from the desk and handed it to him. "This is the current list of things that need to be done around here. The most important is putting together the crib for Ms. Lilly. I keep one in case I get an infant." She shot him a wistful smile. "It's been over a year since I've had a baby in the house. Most of the kids I get are older."

"I can put it together. No problem."

"Great. Then there's the kitchen window and the replacement of the fence in the south pasture. The one out there right now is falling down and dangerous. The wood for the new fence was delivered yesterday. It's behind the barn and covered with a blue tarp. If you want to make that the third thing on your priority list, that would be great."

"Of course." He tapped his hand with the paper, then met her gaze. "I'll understand if you want to rescind your offer."

"I don't." She smiled. "Oh, one more thing. We have an annual event called A Day at The Ranch. It's a combination of amateur rodeo, calf roping, too much food, and lots of games for the kids. The whole town usually comes out and we have a blast while raising money for the ranch—which is registered as a nonprofit. I can tell you more about that later, but everything is coming up fast, so I wanted you to be aware there's a ton of work to do."

"Then we'll get it done."

"Excellent. Thank you." She blew out a sigh. Some of the heavy stress she'd been weighted down with slid from her shoulders. "Well, now that we've got that taken care of, I'm going to head into town to get a few things. Anything you need while I'm there?"

"No, nothing. Thanks." He looked slightly dazed by the fact that she hadn't sent him on his way, but then he cleared his throat and rose. "I'll board up the kitchen window and get that crib put together while you're gone, then get started on the fence." He paused. "Unless you'd like for me to go with you?"

"No, that's okay. Regina and Grant seemed to think if the guy shows up again, it'll be here. I'm probably safer in town than staying here, so I think we'll be fine. And I've already called Gary Knight, who owns the glass place in town. He's going to send someone out to replace the pane. He said it might be tomorrow before he could get out here, though, so plywood will work for now."

Mac nodded and stood. "All right."

"I think I'm also going to pick up one of those systems that have cameras you can monitor on your phone. At least until someone can get out here to put a more sophisticated system in. But at least there'll be cameras."

"That's a good idea. Just having those in sight might be a good deterrent."

"Exactly what I was thinking."

"All right. You be careful. You have my number if you need something."

"Of course."

He turned to leave then stopped and nodded to the framed diploma on the wall. "You're a doctor?"

"Of psychiatry."

"And you run a ranch and take in foster kids."

"Like I said, I understand the need for change." She shrugged. "I was at a private practice for a while, but Josiah and I had dreams that involved this ranch and kids who needed to know someone loved them."

"I see. That's very admirable. You think you'll ever go back to private practice?"

"Maybe one day. For now, I believe I'm doing what I'm supposed to be doing."

"Then that's all that counts. Be careful driving into town."

He disappeared through the door and she stared at the empty space for a moment. Why did having his number give her such a good feeling? Why did his telling her to be careful give her warm fuzzies? And what was it about him that had drawn her to him so fast? The fact that his first instinct was to protect her and chase down the intruder this morning? Or the fact that he tried to hide the pain she sensed lurking beneath his serious surface?

She sighed and rubbed her eyes. It didn't really matter. She needed help and he was there to do it. That was all that she needed to worry about right now. Her phone buzzed. "Hello?"

"Hey, this is Cheryl. We should be finished with the doctor in another fifteen minutes or so. I need to get Lilly dropped off with you ASAP and get out to another call."

"Okay, I was heading into town anyway to grab a few things. I'll meet you at the doctor's office and pick her up."

"Perfect. And Isabelle?"

"Yes?"

"Be careful." The deep seriousness in the woman's voice tightened Isabelle's nerves. "I'm not positive, but I think I saw someone sitting on a motorcycle outside the doctor's office, watching."

"Did you call the police?"

"I did. By the time they got here, the guy was gone and we were back in a room."

"Okay, thanks for the heads-up."

She hung up and headed for her van, her mind spinning. It had been an exciting morning, to say the least. And now this? She couldn't help wondering what she was getting herself into.

Mac walked to the window of the room that Isabelle had designated as the nursery. Small enough to be considered a large closet, it would suffice for as long as Lilly needed a place to sleep. From his position, he watched Isabelle climb into the Honda Odyssey and shut the door. Once her taillights disappeared around the curve near the end of the drive, he pulled the parts of the crib from the closet and laid them out on the floor along with the directions.

His heart pounded at the sight of the pieces, the memories taking him back almost two years to a time he'd done his best to forget. A time of happiness and anticipation that had been wiped away in a single night. "Why, God? I just wish I could understand why."

When the familiar silence descended, Mac backed from the room and raced out of the house. Cody Ray looked up from where he was trimming one of the bushes back from the porch. "Everything okay?"

"Yeah." Milo and Sugar sprinted over, butting him and asking for ear scratches. Mac obliged, even as he breathed in deep, wrestling his emotions into submission. "Uh…yeah. Just trying to figure out which thing is the priority. Putting the crib together or boarding up the kitchen window."

"I'd say the window. Supposed to rain this afternoon."

"Right. Thanks. I'll go take care of that now." He could do that without having a breakdown. Hopefully. He gave the dogs one more pat.

"Got some plywood in the barn. Leaning up against the wall next to the saddles. Do you want me to grab it?"

"I can do it."

"Tools and nails are on the workbench just outside the office. You'll spot them." Cody Ray went back to his snipping.

"Thanks."

Boarding up the window took him all of fifteen minutes once he had the Skilsaw set up, and for every one of those minutes, he never stopped thinking of the pretty widow with the gaggle of children. She'd captured his attention in a way that hadn't been done since—well, *since*. Suffice it to say it had been a long time. He nailed the last corner in place, then turned to look out over the pasture in the direction the guy had run this morning. The officers hadn't bothered to go look for the guy once Mac returned to tell them he'd seen him hop on a motorcycle and ride away toward the highway beyond the woods.

But…

"Hey, Cody Ray!"

"Yeah?" The man had moved to the bush on the other side of the porch.

"I'm going to go check something out in the woods. I'll be right back, okay?"

"You need any help?"

"No, I'm good. Thanks."

"Sure thing. Just watch out for Duke."

Mac stopped. "Duke?"

"The bull. He's always in the back pasture near the tree line. Isabelle keeps him there because he can be temperamental and she doesn't want the kids near him. She's got a buyer coming out sometime this week to take him off her hands. Until then, he's banished and the kids are forbidden to go near him."

"Good to know. I'll keep an eye out for Duke."

Mac jogged to the tree line and stopped just inside the wooded area. Just like he'd done a few hours earlier. He walked the path he'd run and scanned the ground, hoping to see something. Anything that might help him figure out who the hooded figure was.

It had rained two days before, and while the pasture had mostly dried in the sun, the ground beneath his feet was still damp. He remembered the patch of mud that had almost taken him down and continued to trek his way toward it.

When he arrived at the spot, he stopped and scoured the area. A piece of fabric on a branch captured his attention. He pulled his phone from his pocket and snapped a picture. It sure looked like the color of the hoodie the guy had on. He'd leave it there and let the officers know to retrieve it.

Further inspection finally paid off and he found a partial boot print that didn't belong to him. He took another picture. A few steps later, he knelt and gave a grunt of satisfaction. "That will help." The guy had rolled the bike a few short steps before climbing on and roaring away. That meant the tire print was nice and clean. He added that picture to the other two.

A rustle to his left stilled him. The wind was blowing, but that wasn't a "wind" sound. "Anyone there?"

The snap of a branch, the huff of a breath.

"Hey!" Mac automatically reached for the weapon he didn't carry anymore and dropped his hand. He walked toward the noises, then hesitated. Could be a bear. They were popular in this area. Bear or two-legged creature with a weapon? He wasn't crazy about facing either while he was unarmed.

"What are you doing out here?"

Mac spun, heart racing. He pressed a hand to his chest and choked out a short laugh at the sight of Officer Regina Jacobson. "Way to scare a guy to death. I'm looking for evidence." Had it been her he'd heard? But the noises had come from the other side of him. And it was quite possible he was still on edge from this morning and the noises were nothing to be alarmed about. "Hold on a second." He pushed through the bushes and trees to see what the noise could have been—and startled a deer. The buck ran off and Mac shook his head. He returned to Regina. "What are you doing?"

"The same as you. I got to thinking we should have at least checked the place over, so I came back to do it. Cody told me where to find you."

"Right. Well, since you're here, I don't suppose you have any evidence bags on you."

"I do." She pulled one out of her pocket. "One thing I've learned being a small-town cop—always be prepared and up to date on everything just like the bigger departments."

"You take a lot of continuing ed classes?"

"Oh, yeah. The sheriff is on top of all the latest crime-fighting stuff and insists his officers do the same."

That made him feel a lot better. Mac directed her to the scrap of material. "I think it matches the hoodie he had on."

"If we find him and the hoodie, guess we can know for sure."

"There's a partial boot print and a really good tire print you could get a mold of."

"I have the stuff in my cruiser. I'll do that." She hesitated. "You realize this is a long shot."

"Of course." He shrugged. "But I've always found having the evidence is better than not."

"You were in law enforcement." It wasn't a

question. She replaced her black gloves with evidence collection ones before gathering and tucking the piece of cloth into the bag.

He shot her a tight smile. "A few years ago."

"Why'd you get out?"

"For various reasons." He had no intention of sharing his past with someone he'd just met. Not even if she was a cop. "You've known Isabelle for a long time," he said.

She nodded. "We went to school together. She stole my Jello in first grade, and I punched her in the eye. We've been best friends ever since."

He laughed. "That's a great story. Glad to see you two worked out your differences."

She smiled. "I'll be right back."

Mac rubbed a hand over his forehead and considered whether to call Isabelle and let her know what he'd found. Then decided against it. No need to distract her or remind her of the incident while she was out shopping. That wasn't his job or his place. He'd let Regina fill her in.

But he couldn't help hoping the evidence would lead to a quick apprehension, because his gut kept sending warning signals that there was more to come with the man who'd been here earlier.

And it wasn't going to be good.

THREE

Isabelle had picked up Lilly from Cheryl, who reported that the doctor had given the infant a clean bill of health. Now she pushed her full grocery buggy to the checkout line and sent up a prayer Lilly's congenial temperament would last just a little while longer. But the baby had already started fussing. "Hang on, sweetie. I'm almost done, I promise. Then we'll get you home for a bottle and a nap. Okay?"

Her first stop had resulted in some cute outfits for Lilly, a couple of toys, and a baby swing for half price. It had been a while since she'd had an infant placed in her care—well over a year—but most of what she needed was at the house. Unfortunately, her second stop for the security cameras had been a bust, but they were now on order and should arrive two days from now.

Movement to her left distracted her once more and she turned to see a young man wearing a hoodie duck his head and grab a bag of chips from the end cap. Did he have a goatee? She thought she might have seen a flash of one but wasn't positive. A chill skated up her spine. Was that the guy who'd tried to break into her house this morning?

She looked away while her heart pounded. Should she confront him? With one hand on the baby's foot, Isabelle looked back.

He was gone.

A low breath escaped her. She was just paranoid. It was cold. A lot of people wore hoodies this time of year and baseball caps were year-round head attire. She glanced at other shoppers and spotted several people wearing them. The person in front of her finished paying and pushed her buggy toward the exit.

While Isabelle unloaded the items from her own cart onto the belt, she scanned the store once more.

And saw him again. This time in the checkout line three rows down. She curled her fingers around her phone.

"Isabelle? Is that you?"

Isabelle jerked her gaze to the woman in line behind her. "Oh, Valerie. Hey, how are you doing?" Valerie Lovett. Valerie's husband, Travis, and Isabelle's late husband, Josiah, had been best friends before Josiah was killed in a motorcycle accident two years ago.

The woman shrugged. "I'm fine." She nodded to the baby. "I see you have a new addition to your team."

"This is Lilly. She arrived this morning."

"She's a cutie." Valerie shook her head. "I sure do admire you. As much as I love them, I don't want any more. I can't wait to send my two off to school each morning."

"But you're glad to see them when they come home."

"Well, yes. That fact does make me feel less of a bad mother."

"You're a wonderful mom—and Realtor. Sell any houses lately?" Valerie and Travis owned one of the top real estate companies based in Timber Creek.

She laughed. "Not today, but I've got a few things in the works, so hopefully sometime next week, I'll see a sale. Travis had a good one a few days ago and said he has a surprise for me."

"What kind of surprise?"

"I'm not sure." She shrugged. "Who knows with him? I hope it's not something expensive."

"He does like his toys, doesn't he?"

Valerie scowled. "He does. And he spends way too much on them." She sighed. "Then again, I knew that when I married him, so I guess I can't whine about it."

"Very true, my friend." Isabelle smiled and spotted a family she didn't know. "Seems like more and more people move here every month."

"Can you blame them? This is a gorgeous town." Valerie wiggled her brows. "And I'm not complaining about the influx—or the rising property values."

Isabelle smiled. "I'm grateful the land I have was a wedding gift from my parents. I'd never be able to afford that place otherwise."

"The JoBelle Ranch was their dream as much as yours and you know it."

"I do." Lilly let out a low cry and Isabelle pulled a stuffed toy from her bag and passed it to the baby. Lilly took it and stuffed it in her mouth.

"Speaking of your parents," Valerie said, "how's your mother doing since her fall?"

Isabelle grimaced. "I haven't talked to her today, but it's on my list. Yesterday, Dad said he had his work cut out for himself keeping Mom in bed." Her mother had been helping her father with a horse when she'd stepped wrong and gone down, breaking her hip and foot in the process. Her dad, who'd taken over a lot of the ranch duties after Josiah was killed, had been suddenly thrust into the role of full-time caregiver.

Hence the need for her to hire Mac. The thought of the handsome newcomer almost made her smile. Almost.

"...need anything, please let me know."

Isabelle blinked. She'd zoned out for a moment, but caught most of what Valerie had said. "Thanks, I appreciate it."

"Ma'am, do you want help with your groceries?"

"Yes, please." Having the bagger escort her to the van wasn't something she was going to turn down. She glanced around, looking for the man that had shaken her nerves. When she didn't see him, she wasn't sure whether to be relieved or more worried. Isabelle waved to her friend and followed the young teen who pushed the cart. Lilly seemed to like the view of the new face and babbled at him.

He babbled back, and just like that, Lilly was smitten. Isabelle laughed. "You must have younger brothers or sisters," Isabelle said.

"Three. My youngest sister just turned two."

"Well, you've definitely got a way with little ones."

While the two of them carried on their conversation, Isabelle kept an eye on the surroundings. She didn't see anyone that raised the hair on her neck—or the young man from the grocery store—but the parking lot was crowded, and she couldn't see into every vehicle. The good thing was, she didn't see any motorcycles in the lot.

While the grocery worker loaded the items into the back of the van, she made sure Lilly was safely strapped into what was now her spot in the van.

"Thank you, ma'am," the teen said. "Bye, Lilly, come back soon."

He waved and jogged back toward the store while Isabelle climbed into the driver's seat and locked the doors. With one last look around, she cranked the van and made her way out of the lot.

When no one followed, she breathed a low sigh of relief and headed home. Shortly into the fifteen-minute drive, Lilly decided she was done. Her wails lifted from the back, tuning up like a tornado siren. "Oh, baby, I'm sorry. I tried to hurry, but I guess I wasn't fast enough. We'll be home soon."

The cries grew louder, and while Isabelle knew the child was perfectly safe strapped in her seat, the infant's unhappiness broke her heart. She remembered the note and turned on the radio to a soothing jazz station. For a moment, it had no effect on the sobs, but then the shrieks slowed, and finally morphed into hiccups.

"Okay," she whispered, "thank you, baby's mommy, for the note."

The steering wheel pulled to the right. She spun it back. And then a low *thump, thump, thump* finally penetrated her rattled brain and she realized she had a flat. "Oh, seriously? Now? I just had these tires put on last month." She wasn't sure who she was talking to, but saying the words out loud helped her keep it together. And then Lilly let out more demanding wails. Isabelle raked a hand over her head. "Great. Just fabulous."

She maneuvered the van over to the side of the road and put it in Park. The thought of changing the tire completely deflated her. She smirked at her unintentional pun but couldn't quite work up to a laugh. Instead, she groaned. "I do not want to deal with this." Josiah had made sure she knew how to do it; she just didn't want to have to do it and try to take care of Lilly at the same time.

Part of the reason the baby was cranky was because it was time for her to eat again. Isabelle had pushed too hard in her effort to wait until they got home to feed her. "Okay, baby, I'll feed you, and hopefully, you'll go to sleep and I can change the tire while you sleep."

Or she could just call her dad to come help. But then he'd have to leave her mother. Or she could call Cody Ray. She glanced at the time and winced. The bus with the kids would be arriving any minute now. She drew in a deep breath. She could do this.

She grabbed her phone and stepped out of the van, the baby's cries echoing in her ears. She opened the side door, quickly mixed the formula in the bottle of water and shook it. "Okay, sweetie, here you go." Lilly latched on as though she was starving and went to work on making the formula disappear.

Isabelle called Cody Ray and got his voice mail. "All righty, then. Let's try Mac."

He answered on the second ring. "Hello?"

"It's Isabelle."

"Everything okay?"

"Oh, just peachy." She filled him in. "I'm going to be a little later than I planned. Could you make sure Cody Ray meets the school bus and gets the kids settled? He knows the routine. It's going to take me at least thirty minutes to get this tire changed."

"I'm on my way."

"No, Mac, it's fine. I can—"

"Hey, Cody Ray! Can you meet the kids at the bus? I need to go help Isabelle."

Cody Ray's affirmative response reached her. "Mac—" The slamming of the truck door told her protesting was futile. "Okay, thanks. We'll be right here. I'll just share my location with you and you should be able to drive straight here." She tapped the screen to navigate to the place where she could send him her location just as the roar of a motorcycle heading her way sent shivers crawling up her spine. "Oh, no."

"Isabelle?"

Okay, she knew there was more than one motorcycle in the town of Timber Creek, but…

The bike drew closer and Isabelle slammed the van's side door, climbed into the driver's seat and hit the locks.

"Isabelle? Talk to me. What's going on?" Mac's worried voice came through the line.

"I think the guy on the motorcycle is back."

Isabelle's shaky statement echoed in his mind. "I'm seven minutes away," Mac said. "Where is he?"

"Coming up behind us. I may just be paranoid, but I don't want to take any chances. I've locked us in the van."

"Of course."

"He's probably going to go right past us."

"Let's hope so. Do you have a gun?"

"At home, locked in the gun safe."

Now Mac could hear the engine of the bike approaching. And slowing. "Isabelle?"

"He's not going past, Mac. He's stopping."

"Do you have any kind of weapon in your car?"

Her breathing came quickly over the line. "No." A slight pause. "Wait. I have a baseball bat."

"Then get it and be prepared to use it. If he keeps his helmet on, go for his stomach or the knees. Or whatever you can hit. Can you do that?"

Her hesitation worried him. "Yes," she finally said. "I could do it to protect Lilly or one of the kids. He's not going to hurt her if I can help it."

The steel in her voice told him everything he needed to know. "Tell me what he's doing now. I'm four minutes away."

"He's just sitting there."

"Sounds like he's trying to decide what to do. Be prepared for him to do anything, okay?"

She went silent.

"Keep talking to me, Isabelle. I don't like not hearing your voice."

"You mean you can't hear my heart beating hard enough to jackhammer concrete?"

Her breathless joke tightened his throat for some reason. "Yeah. And that's completely normal."

"He's walking behind his bike and opening something. Mac, what if he's getting a gun? Bullets go through glass."

He was aware.

He heard her start the van engine. "I'm going to have to try to drive on this flat tire."

"Do what you have to do. I'm getting closer. Anyone else on the road?"

"No, just me for now, but I'm worried about someone else coming along. This guy could do anything." She paused. "He's walking this way and he's carrying something. I think it's a hammer."

"Stop!" Mac heard the yelled order from a voice he didn't recognize and figured Isabelle had pressed the gas.

"What do you want?" Isabelle cried.

Mac gripped the wheel and accelerated as much as he dared. He couldn't go much faster on the winding road without risking going over the edge.

"He's chasing me! I have two flat tires, Mac. I can't get away from him!"

The sound of breaking glass reached him, and Isabelle's scream sent terror racing through his veins.

FOUR

Isabelle had ducked when she'd seen him lift the hammer, but he'd released it quickly, sending it through the window and clipping her forehead. A shriek had escaped her when the hammer landed in the passenger seat. Pain radiated through her skull and her foot slipped from the gas pedal. The phone tumbled to the floorboard. "Oh, God, please protect us. Please."

Blood from the wound blinded her for a moment before she swiped a hand across her left eye and tried to keep watch on her attacker.

Lightheaded and nauseous, tension threaded through her while her adrenaline flowed. The motorcycle rider loped toward her, his outstretched hand grasping the door handle and yanking. His yell at finding the door locked pulled Isabelle from her shock and she slammed her foot on the gas.

His hand slipped and he fell back with a howl of frustration and anger. The van lurched and she fought with the wheel to keep it on the road. The cold wind whipped in through the broken driver's window, slapping her ponytail around her aching head.

But just ahead, she caught sight of Mac's truck barreling toward her.

A hard hand reached through the broken window and clamped onto her ponytail. Another scream ripped from her throat and she slammed on the brake. The van's abrupt halt sent the man crashing into the door. His hand fell from her hair, and she swung the ball bat toward the window only to find him gone. In the rearview mirror, she could see him running full out back to his motorcycle.

"Isabelle!"

Mac reached the van. Isabelle shot a quick glance at the baby. Lilly's eyes were wide, but she had the bottle still clamped between her lips. She was fine. They were both fine and still alive. Isabelle flung the door open. Without thought, she threw herself into Mac's arms, only halfway believing he was really there. When she realized what she was doing, she jerked back. "I'm sorry. I'm just really glad to see you. Yet again, you have impeccable timing. Thank you."

"Of course. Are you all right?" He lifted a hand to touch the wound and she leaned back. He dropped his hand.

"Sorry, I'll be fine. Head wounds bleed a lot, right?"

"So I've heard. Looks like it grazed you, but you still need to see the doctor."

Her head pounded harder at the thought, but she nodded. "I'll call Katherine when I get home."

"Katherine?"

"One of the town's doctors and a friend to me and the children. Actually, I'll send her a heads-up text. She may need me to come by her office back in town."

"I don't hear any noise coming from the van. I take it Lilly's all right?"

"Yes."

She punched the message into her phone only to get an automated reply that her friend was out of town at a conference for the next two days.

She grimaced and slid the van's side door open to discover Lilly had finished her bottle and drifted off to sleep. "She had a big morning. I guess a hammer through the window and a scary motorcycle rider weren't on her list of things to worry about today."

"Let's be thankful for the little things." He shook his phone at her. "I think I can hang up now?"

She let out a short laugh. "I think so. Katherine's not in the office, so I'll just take some ibuprofen when I get home."

He pursed his lips as he hung up and dialed the sheriff's number. Isabelle listened as he reported the incident. Then, while he worked on transferring the groceries and Lilly to the back seat of his king cab, Isabelle snagged her phone and looked up the number for her roadside assistance. After arranging for the tow truck to pick up her van and take it to the shop for repair of her almost new tires and a window, she climbed in the passenger seat and buckled up.

Once they were finally on the road, she closed her eyes, only to have the images of her attack hit her full force. Her eyes popped open. "I don't understand what this guy wants and why he keeps coming after me. It's got to be the baby."

"I don't know, either, but it's definitely not random. And since your doctor friend's not around, I'm taking you to the hospital to get that head looked at."

"What?" He'd managed to turn around and head back toward town without her realizing it. "No. I really don't think I need a doctor. It's just a graze."

"It's still bleeding."

"Head wounds bleed."

He handed her a package of tissues from the pocket in the door. "Isabelle, if you wind up with a concussion or something, who's going to take care of the children?"

She fell silent. He was right. She was the children's designated caretaker, and if something happened to her, Child Protection would step in and take away the kids. Everyone that worked for her had to have a background check, but she was the only one certified to foster. "Okay, fine. But I need to call Cody Ray and let him know."

She placed the call, and after assuring the worried man she was okay and that this was just a checkup, she hung up and eyed Mac. "Happy?"

"On that subject, yes. Next question. Is there anyone in your life that you've recently made mad?"

She groaned. She stopped dabbing the head wound and just pressed the tissues to it. "No, not that I can think of, anyway. The parents of the kids who've been removed from their homes probably aren't very happy with me, but they don't know who I am. At least I don't think they do. They're not supposed to."

He cut his gaze to her and then back to the road as he navigated the twists and turns. "Do you know how easy it would be for someone to find out where their kid went?"

Isabelle grimaced. "Yes. I know. I've never really worried about it before, but now I'm wondering if one of them managed to track me down." She frowned. "But why come after me? Why not just grab your kid and hit the road? I mean, it would be horrible if that actually happened, but...why not?" She paused. "Unless that's what the guy was trying to do. Grab Lilly."

"Because he left her and had second thoughts?"

"Yes."

"That's one theory. Could also be a revenge thing."

"Revenge? Maybe." But she didn't think so. She called Regina and asked her to meet her at the emergency room entrance so she could make the report.

Mac pulled into the hospital's parking lot and she bit her lip, trying to think of what she might have done to set someone on the path of revenge. Raising their kid when they couldn't? Yes, that could spark a deep anger.

By the time he parked, she was no closer to figuring it out than when she'd started. A police cruiser sat in the police parking space at the entrance, and when Isabelle stepped out of Mac's truck, Regina opened the door of the vehicle. "Are you sure you're okay?"

"I have a monster headache that may or may not have anything to do with the hammer and everything to do with how my day has been going.

But I'm not complaining. It would have been so much worse if Mac hadn't—once again—come to the rescue." She lowered the soiled tissues and frowned when Regina's eyes went wide.

"Let's get you seen," her friend said. "Quickly."

Lilly was still asleep when Mac lifted her carrier out of the back of the cab. "I've got her and the bag."

"I'll need a statement from you, too," Regina said.

"Of course." He led the way into the hospital waiting room. Regina's presence seemed to speed things up a bit, and Isabelle soon found herself seated on an exam table having her vitals taken. Mac sat in the chair across from her, the carrier on the floor between his feet. She couldn't help noticing the shadows that darkened his eyes whenever he looked at the baby. And yet, his features also held a tenderness that tugged at her heart.

Regina pulled out the same little black notebook from that morning. "All right. Tell me the details."

Isabelle let out another groan and talked until the doctor entered the room and pronounced her fine—except for the three stitches his nurse would be putting in.

Regina patted her hand. "I'll be outside to give you an escort home when you're done."

* * *

Mac carried the baby into the house and set her carrier on the floor next to the sofa. The little girl from the morning—Katie—came running from the kitchen, still clutching her doll, and launched herself at Isabelle just inside the door. Isabelle went to her knees to catch the mini missile.

"Izzy-belle," Katie said, "are you okay? Mr. Cody said you had to go see the doctor." She touched Isabelle's head with the gentleness of a butterfly. "You hurted your head."

Isabelle hugged the child, and Mac had to look away thanks to the lump that grew in his throat. He honestly didn't know if he had the strength to stay and do this job. Not if he had to be around the children for any length of time and being constantly reminded of everything he'd lost. But today had been weird. During a typical day, he could probably avoid them and the pain they triggered. He cleared his throat. "I think I'll go get that crib put together then get started on the fence."

Isabelle kissed Katie on the cheek, then rose. "Just in case you want to know the evening schedule around here, we always eat dinner at six." She tilted her head. "That's Ms. Sybil you hear banging around in the kitchen. Then I'll get Katie ready for bed while the older kids work on their homework and have an hour of down-time before they do showers and bed. You're welcome to join us for dinner or do your own thing—which you can do since I purchased a few groceries for you."

He blinked. "You didn't have to do that."

"Just a few staples to say welcome. It was the least I could do—especially after you've come to my rescue twice in one day. I'll put the groceries in your kitchen if you'd like, or I can keep them in my fridge until you're ready to get them."

He didn't know what to say. "That's…really kind. Thank you."

"You're welcome. So…your kitchen or mine?"

He laughed. "Mine works. Thanks."

"Who's this?" A new voice asked from the doorway of the kitchen. And older woman in her early sixties stood there, trying her hands on a towel.

"This is Mac," Isabelle said. "Mac, this is Sybil."

"*Ms.* Sybil," Katie corrected.

Mac smiled. "Nice to meet you, *Ms.* Sybil." He emphasized her name exactly as Katie had done. The child beamed at him. "I'm headed to work on that crib now. If I'm late, don't wait dinner for me."

"Of course," Isabelle said. The smile didn't quite reach her eyes and he had a feeling she was barely holding it together. But it wasn't his business. She'd hired him to put the crib together and fix her fence. So that was what he'd do. He walked out the door and headed for the barn to grab a few tools. He refused to turn around to ask her one more time if she was all right.

But he had to admit he was bothered. By the pretty foster mom and the fact that someone had come after her twice now. That thought raised his blood pressure more than a fraction. He hesitated, sighed and walked back to the house, up the steps and knocked on the front door. Katie answered it. "Hiya, Mr. Mac. Whatcha doing? Thought you were gonna to fix Lily's crib."

His heart tumbled all over itself at the innocence shining in those bright gray eyes. "I am. Soon. I just wanted to ask Isabelle a quick question." For a brief moment, he wondered what Katie's story was and how she'd come to live with Isabelle, but he pushed the thought aside. If he got to know the people here, he'd start to care. And he couldn't afford to do that, since he'd be leaving as soon as he had some money saved up. He was so close to his goal—enough money for the down payment on some land he'd picked out. He couldn't get sidetracked now.

"She went out the kitchen door. I think she

was going to the barn for a minute. Sometimes she likes to visit Maverick."

"Who's Maverick?"

Katie giggled. "Her horse, silly."

"Oh, right. Of course." He patted her on the head. "Thanks, kiddo."

"You're welcome. You going to find her?"

Nosy little thing, wasn't she? "Yes, like I said, I want to ask her a question."

"Okay. Isabelle likes horses."

Chatty, too. "I do, too."

"Are you a good rider?"

"I am. Are you?"

"No, I'm learning, though. I like roping better."

She was quite the conversationalist. "Well, I guess I'd better—"

"Do you know how to rope?"

"I do."

"Did you see Duke?"

"Duke?" Why was he supposed to know that name? "Oh, the bull?"

"Yes. He's mean." She scrunched up her face and blew air out of her nose. Then pawed the ground with her right foot like she was going to charge him at any moment. It was all Mac could do to hold it together and not burst out laughing. "That's what he does if you get close to him," Katie said. "I stay far-r-r-r-r away. You should, too."

"Thank you. I'll do that."

"Katie?" Ms. Sybil's voice came from the kitchen.

"I'm coming! Bye, Mr. Mac." She shut the door before Mac could respond. He allowed himself a quick smile that morphed into a chuckle. The sound was rusty and surprised him, but his steps were lighter than they'd been in a long time. He hurried to round the house and head for the barn. Cody Ray was nowhere to be seen when Mac stepped into the chilly interior. He stood still for a moment and let his eyes adjust. Fluorescent lights burned overhead and he caught sight of Isabelle at the end of the row of stalls.

Horses nickered at him as he passed, but he didn't stop to introduce himself. Isabelle's forehead was pressed against the neck of the horse, and her shoulders shook, but no sound reached him.

Mac stopped, realizing he was intruding on an extremely private moment. He paused, wondering if he should leave before she noticed him, or offer what little comfort he could.

He'd just opted to leave when she raised her head, her eyes colliding with his. "Oh. Mac. I didn't… I'm sorry." She scrubbed the tears from her cheeks, leaving her skin red and splotchy.

"No, no. I should apologize. I was just getting ready to leave you alone when you looked up."

A weary sigh slipped from her. "It's okay. I come here sometimes when I need to have a little breakdown. Then I get myself together and can be around people once more."

"I would say after a day like today, you're entitled to a breakdown."

She laughed. A watery one that ended on a hiccup. "Maybe so, but I'm done now. I need to get myself cleaned up and feed the baby. I also have to make a few phone calls before I can mark this day done."

"Anything I can do to help?" The words left his lips of their own volition. What was it about Isabelle that had him throwing eighteen months of emotional-wall building to the wayside?

"No, but thank you. The phone calls are about the Day at the Ranch event coming up. I think everything is basically set up, but there are always last-minute fires to put out." She headed for the door then turned back. "Oh, did you need something?"

"No. Not really. You looked upset and I thought I'd just make sure you were okay."

Her eyes softened, and she gave him a slight nod. "Thank you. That's very kind of you."

"Sure. Well... I'll leave you to it, then. Go put out your fires."

The smile she shot him seemed to come easier and her features a little more relaxed. When she passed him, the fruity scent of her shampoo lingered behind her and he couldn't help drawing in a deep breath.

He watched her go, thinking she was too young to have all this responsibility heaped on her slender shoulders. She shouldn't have to do all of this alone. "Don't do it, Mac," he muttered. "Don't get involved. Her problems are not yours. And besides, she's not really alone. She's got Cody Ray and Ms. Sybil."

Vocalizing the words didn't change a thing. Especially not his desire to help the pretty widow. With a sigh, he headed for the fence, glad he'd be able to see the house from where he'd be working.

But while his head might order him to stay uninvolved, he was pretty sure his heart wasn't listening.

FIVE

Four days had passed with no more intruders or scary people throwing hammers through her van's window. In fact, the van had been fixed and now sat in the driveway in front of the house. She had a new windowpane in her kitchen, a new security system that she was scared to death she'd forget how to work, and all seemed to have returned to normal.

But Isabelle couldn't relax—or sleep. In spite of her exhaustion, she sat in the swing on the front porch in the early-morning chill, coffee cup in hand, while she watched the sun rise. She loved this time of day and took advantage of the quiet as often as possible to spend time praying, asking God for strength and wisdom.

This morning, she also kept an eye on the tree line for the man who'd attacked her. She kept waiting for him to come back and try again, but so far, no one had. A shiver skated up her spine and a surge of anger tightened her jaw. She refused to let the attacks steal these moments.

The door at the end of the porch opened and boots hit the wooden planks. Immediately, her pulse slowed and her heart lightened.

"Morning," Mac said.

"Good morning."

His first morning at the ranch he'd found her in her spot and had joined her every morning since before heading out to ride the property, looking for fences that needed repairing, or helping Cody Ray in the barn. This morning, she knew he planned to move the cattle in the lower pasture to the upper, where there was more grass. She sent up a silent prayer of thanks for Mac's arrival. He was the help she'd prayed for after her mother's fall and her father's necessary absence.

He sat in the white wooden rocker and sipped the steaming brew from the blue mug. "It's going to be a pretty day."

"My favorite kind." Isabelle would admit that the more she was around Mac, the more she wanted to know him. But he was a hard one to figure out. She sensed pain in his past and wondered about it.

He rocked for a moment, then leaned forward. "You ever hear anything from your cop friend, Regina, about the evidence she sent off?"

"That piece of material?" She shook her head. "She said they were checking for DNA, I don't think the results have come back from the lab yet."

"Not surprising. It can take a while." The sun peeked over the horizon and the normal peaceful feeling Isabelle gleaned from the majestic sight was missing today. It was hard to find peace when nightmares stalked her rest.

"How's Lilly sleeping?"

"Better the last two nights. I hope she's not keeping you awake." The baby was a restless sleeper and had yet to make it through the night without waking up crying.

"No. I hear her every so often, but your walls are thick. I can just roll over and go back to sleep." He frowned. "If you ever want me to take a night getting up with her so you can get a decent night's sleep, I'm happy to do it."

His concern pierced her. "Thank you, that's very kind of you, but you've got the ranch to keep up with. I'll manage with Lilly. She's just adjusting and will settle down eventually." He studied her and Isabelle felt heat climbing into her cheeks. "What?"

"Nothing. You do a good job with these kids. They adore you."

She blinked at the praise, then smiled. "Thanks.

The feeling's mutual. Give them a chance and they'll adore you, too."

"Hmm."

Sounds from the kitchen pulled Isabelle to her feet. "I guess that's my cue."

He nodded and took a sip of his coffee, his eyes thoughtful. Shadowed. One day, she wanted to hear what had put the sadness there, but that story would have to wait. She had kids to take care of. A smile tilted her lips upward. Then faded as she stepped into the house. Not only did she need to take care of the kids, she needed to protect them.

Please, God, help me take care of and protect these children. They have no one else but us. With that prayer on her lips, she hurried to take the baby from Ms. Sybil. At the kitchen window, she stared out toward the wooded area, wondering if the man was out there, watching and waiting.

Her arms tightened around Lilly and she couldn't help wondering if the baby was the reason for the sudden attacks. She kissed the infant's head. "Don't worry, baby girl, they'll have to go through me to get to you. I promise."

Mac waved to the children as they loaded up on the bus to head to school. From his spot along the fence, he faced the left side of the house. He could see the driveway to his right and the woods behind the pasture to his left. Just on the other side of the woods was one of the back roads that led to town. Beyond that, the wooded area rose sharply and blended into a majestic mountain view. Very soothing and peaceful.

When intruders weren't trying to break in.

In fact, the area was almost as beautiful as the place he'd picked out when he decided he was ready to settle down. And he was getting there. The pain of his losses was still there, but it wasn't as sharp or debilitating.

Mac turned his attention back to hammering nails into the new wood. The fence would definitely take him several more days to finish. He'd get a few of the boards up, then he'd head over and help Cody Ray muck out the stalls, lay fresh hay, and fill up the troughs out in the pasture.

He could see why Isabelle had needed help ASAP. Cody Ray was a hardworking man, but he couldn't take care of the place by himself.

A pang of regret sliced through Mac. Maybe he shouldn't have applied for this job. Maybe he should have just said no when he realized that Isabelle was going to need someone long-term.

But…he'd been straight up honest with her. She knew he didn't plan on sticking around for an extended period of time. He figured if he stayed for the next two or three months, he'd have more than enough to put a down payment on his own place. Then eventually build the barn to house the horses he'd board...

One step at a time.

A scream from the house pulled Mac up short. "Stop him! He's got the baby!"

Mac gripped the hammer and ran toward the house. He bolted around the side of the porch to see a man racing from the kitchen toward the woods.

He held the carrier tucked against his side. Isabelle flew after him. "Stop! This is kidnapping!"

Mac cut in front of her, his long legs eating up the ground, desperation and adrenaline driving him. "Call the cops!" Mac yelled the order and Isabelle fell back. As he ran, he noted every detail he could see about the guy. Dirty jeans, black shoes, black hoodie. Having to run with the carrier slowed the kidnapper down and Mac gained a lot of ground quickly. He pulled closer.

The man cast a quick look over his shoulder and Mac got a glimpse of a dark goatee and more facial features. In an abrupt move, the kidnapper skidded to a stop and set the carrier down, then took off once again with a fresh burst of speed, disappearing behind the next tree.

Mac drew up short next to the baby. Heart

pounding, he looked down, and his knees went weak when Lilly grinned up at him. At the sound of a motorcycle engine roaring, Mac's jaw tightened. He wanted to try to follow, but there was no way he was leaving Lilly alone. He picked up the carrier and headed back toward the house.

When he entered the kitchen, Isabelle rushed him, reaching for the baby. "Is she okay?"

"Yeah, yeah, she's fine." Mac set the carrier on the table and Isabelle released the child from the restraints and pulled her into her arms. She kissed the fuzz-covered head and Mac's heart thundered with relief—and pain. He swallowed and got a grip on his emotions. Babies and children always brought the past barreling toward him like an out-of-control semi.

"I put her in the carrier," Isabelle said, "because she sounded a little stuffy. I thought she might feel better sitting up. What if I hadn't—"

Mac squeezed her bicep. "She's fine, Isabelle. Really. Focus on that."

"Right. Of course. She's fine and that's all that's important."

He noticed Sybil holding a bag of ice to her head. "Are you all right?"

"I'm fine," the older woman said with a wave of her hand. "He just caught me by surprise is all. If I'd have seen him coming, he never would have gotten close enough to hit me or grab Lilly." She grimaced. "But I had my back to the door."

"I'd walked in just as he snatched the carrier," Isabelle said, "and dashed out the door. And I couldn't… I didn't…"

"It's okay," Mac said. "He had his bike stashed in the woods again."

Isabelle scowled. "This is getting ridiculous."

Mac rubbed his chin and frowned. "How did I miss him? I never saw him come across the pasture."

"The only way he could get to the house without you seeing him," Isabelle said, "is just like he did last time. By coming from the back road through the woods and parking the bike just inside the tree line. Once he got close to the house, he probably saw you working on the fence and simply went around to the cover of the barn."

"Wouldn't Cody Ray have seen him?"

She shook her head. "He rode up to check on the pond in the south pasture. We're going to move some cattle there and he was afraid the water was too low to support them."

"Right," Mac said. "Okay, so the kids are at school and Sybil was in the kitchen with Lilly."

"And I was putting some laundry away," Isabelle said. "So no one would have seen him come from the barn side of the pasture." She sighed. "I don't usually keep the doors locked. When the kids are here, they come and go with all of us keeping an eye on them. When they're outside, Cody Ray watches them if he can. If not, I sit out on the porch. If they're inside, Sybil watches them. I've got to call this in. Again. Regina's going to want to move in with me until this guy is caught."

"That's not a bad idea."

Isabelle gave a low groan and grabbed her cell phone from the counter.

While she dialed, Mac got a pen and paper and wrote down everything he could remember about the man. This time he'd locked eyes with him. The would-be abductor's eyes were blue. And Mac would know them when he saw them again. And he *would* see them again.

Because he'd be looking for them on every face he saw.

SIX

Isabelle had sent Sybil to her home above the garage after being unable to convince the woman she needed to see a doctor. "It's just a goose egg," Sybil had said. "I've had one before and know exactly what the doctor will say. Ice it, ibuprofen for the pain, and rest. I can save my money and do all of that."

"Fine," Isabelle had finally said. "But I'll be checking on you regularly, and if I even suspect you might have a concussion, you're going to the doctor. Understand?"

"Of course, *Mama*."

Isabelle had stuck her tongue out at the woman, who'd chuckled on her way out. That made Isabelle feel a tad better. She took a deep, steadying breath as Regina's cruiser drove into sight. Isabelle locked eyes with Mac. "Regina's here."

"And I'm ready." He waved his paper at her. After Regina finished taking her report at the ranch for the second time in two days, she looked at Isabelle. "I think it's obvious someone is after the baby—and he doesn't care who he has to hurt to get to her. First, he tried to break into the house, then he went after you with the hammer, and now he knocks Ms. Sybil over the head? He's dangerous, Isabelle. And escalating."

"So what do we do? Do I hand Lilly over to you or another stranger and confuse the poor child all over again? She's just getting used to us. She's definitely bonded with me." She swiped a tear that threatened to fall. She'd bonded with Lilly, too, and didn't want to give her up just yet. If ever. But that was a problem for another day. "It's not healthy for her." She huffed a short laugh with no humor. "Of course, being kidnapped isn't, either. But seriously, if I give her over to CPS or the police, whoever is after her will just show up wherever she is." She studied her friend. "Tell me what to do."

"Let me talk to the sheriff," Regina said. "Maybe he can put an officer out here until we can catch this guy."

"You sound doubtful."

A sigh slipped from the officer. "I'm sorry. It's just that we're a little shorthanded right now. The sheriff is looking to hire two more deputies, but so far hasn't found anyone. But this is important. We've got to find a way to keep everyone safe. I'll talk to the sheriff, fill him in on this latest incident, and see what he thinks. I'll also call Cheryl and ask her if she wants to move the kids somewhere else."

Isabelle flinched, but nodded.

Regina snagged her phone from her belt clip. "I'm going to step outside and call. You guys sit tight."

Regina walked out onto the porch and Isabelle turned to Mac. "Are you sure you want to stay? Things are looking pretty crazy right now."

"I'm staying. Now more than ever."

She bit her lip as gratitude rushed through her. "How can I ever repay you?"

"For what? I let him get away."

"But you got Lilly back." She shuddered. "I can't believe he actually came in my house and *grabbed* her with Sybil right there and me in the other room. I mean, it happened so fast my head is still spinning."

"She's safe now. That's all that matters. But I recommend keeping your doors locked from now on."

"Yes. I will. It makes me sad that I have to, but safety is the priority."

Regina stepped back inside. "All right, first, Sheriff Payne said he could spare someone for the next couple of days. Ben Land has been asking for overtime, so he's going to be on his way over shortly."

Isabelle let out a slow breath. "All right. Good. I don't like the fact that it's necessary, but I appreciate the help."

Regina turned to Mac. "Also, you're former law enforcement. Your background check came back clean, so whatever caused you to leave police work wasn't anything illegal."

"No, it wasn't." He shot her a tight smile.

"The sheriff said to ask if you'd do double duty. He said as long as your concealed weapons permit is legit, to get your gun and keep it on you." She paused. "It's legit, right?"

Mac's eyes widened slightly. "Yeah, it is."

"Excellent. Then I feel like everyone out here will be in good hands. I've talked to Cheryl to ask her what she wants to do about the children and she said she has absolutely nowhere else to put the kids. They'd have to go to a whole other location, change schools, and everything. She said as long as the sheriff is handling the safety factor, then she's okay with the kids staying."

Isabelle let out a relieved sigh. "Perfect."

"I've assured Cheryl that every precaution is being taken and the children are safe."

"Yes," Mac said, "yes, they are."

Isabelle was touched at the resolve in his voice. But even she knew that if someone really wanted to get to Lilly, at some point they would succeed.

"Please catch this person, Regina," Isabelle said, her voice soft, pleading. "Lilly's already had a rough start in this world. She needs to be able to depend on us to keep her safe. And the other kids do, too. You know their backgrounds. Every single one of them come from nothing but instability and upheaval. This is their happy place—their healing place. They need what this ranch and those of us who work here give to them."

"Absolutely. I agree."

Isabelle nodded and Regina stuck her notebook in her front pocket. She turned to Mac. "I was thinking. You got a pretty good look at the guy this time, right?"

"Yes."

"Could you work with a sketch artist?"

"Of course."

"Good. This town isn't that big. If we have his picture up around a lot of the busier places, someone will recognize him."

"Sounds like a good idea."

"Perfect. I'll have the artist from Asheville drive over to the station. I'll let you know when he can make it, but he's usually pretty quick. It'll probably be later this afternoon or tomorrow morning."

"No problem. Just let me know when."

"Thank you." She turned to Isabelle. "Are we still on for tomorrow? I don't mind changing locations and meeting you here if you would feel safer, but I know Travis has another meeting right after ours. And Donna will need to get back to her store fairly quickly." Donna Taylor. She owned the bakery on Main Street and planned to donate several cakes and other items for the cake-walk at the fundraiser.

"No, I'll be there. I have to pick up Katie's allergy medication. With the officer and Mac here, Lilly will be safe. And with me in town, I should be safe, too, since the kidnapper would have no reason to come after me if I don't have Lilly with me, right?"

Regina shrugged. "Logically, that makes sense."

"I'm not sure that's a good idea," Mac said with a frown. "I think you should have someone with you in spite of Lilly being here and protected. Why don't I take you into town and I can get a few things I need while I'm there, then bring you home?"

Isabelle echoed his frown. "I appreciate the offer, but you have enough to do here. Not only that, but being a bodyguard wasn't exactly in the job description, and I don't feel right asking you do it."

"You're not asking. I'm offering."

His tone said he wasn't budging. She hesitated, then nodded. "Okay, as long you're sure."

"I'm sure."

Regina studied him. "Why'd you leave law enforcement? I can tell you're a natural."

His eyes went dark and Isabelle wished Regina hadn't asked that question with such bluntness. Then Mac sighed. "A little over eighteen months ago, my wife and two-month-old son were killed in a car accident."

Isabelle gasped and went white. Regina flinched. The words had slipped past his filters, so he might as well finish the basics. "As you can imagine, my whole world shattered and I was an emotional wreck. I couldn't do a job where one mistake could cost my partner's life—or an innocent person's. So I quit— with the invitation to return at any point." He shrugged. "I haven't reached that point yet." But he was getting close. If he could offer to protect a woman and her children, he could go back to police work. The silent admission shook him even while a tiny seed of hope sprouted.

"I'm sorry," Regina said. "I shouldn't have asked. It's none of my business."

"No, you were right to ask. I've been on a journey of healing since I left the force, and my training will serve Isabelle and the children well. I want to do this." Actually, he had a feeling that he *needed* to do this—for his own mental health—but kept that to himself.

For some reason, he felt lighter than he had in ages. Telling them about Jeanie and Little Mac set something free inside him. Something he'd have to examine at a later time.

Isabelle still hadn't recovered from his announcement. Her pale features worried him. Just as he was about to ask her if she was all right, she drew in a deep breath. "Well, thank you for sharing that. I'm…actually at a loss for words to say how sorry I am."

Her compassion enveloped him like a warm blanket. "It's been hard. Like I said, it's been a journey, but I'm in a much better place than I was even just a few months ago. So—" he cleared his throat "—tomorrow, I'll follow you into town, you have your meeting, and I'll bring you home. Deal?"

"Deal." She nodded, but he could see the questions swimming in her eyes.

"Would you have time to meet with the sketch artist while you're in town?" Regina asked.

"Of course."

"Good, I'll set it up. I'll give our guy your number and he can tell you when he'll be at the station."

"Sounds good." Mac headed off to get his shoulder holster from his truck. Keeping it hidden from the kids might require some ingenuity, but he'd manage.

For the next several hours, he worked on the fence, then helped Cody Ray in the barn until it was time for the children to get home from school. The police officer, Ben Land, arrived behind the bus. Mac leaned his pitchfork against the side of the barn and walked out into the sunlight just as Katie hopped off the last step of the bus. She spotted him right away and ran over to him. "Hi, Mr. Mac."

His heart pumped a weird beat and he forced a smile even as he crouched to her level. "What's up, pretty girl?"

"Lisa Ann had a birthday party today and she turned six."

"She did, huh? Getting on up there in age, isn't she?"

"I know. She's growing up. Like me." Her gap-toothed grin tugged at his emotions once more. "Anyway," she said, "she broughted cupcakes to school and there was enough for everyone to eat one *and* take one home." She withdrew a slightly smooshed chocolate treat from the top of her backpack. "I tried to keep it safe. Jackie almost sat on it, but I pushed her off the seat."

"You pushed—" He had to duck his head to hide his smile. Then he cleared his throat and looked back up, hoping his expression was appropriately solemn. He caught Isabelle's gaze behind Katie and started. He hadn't heard her walk up. He swept his attention back to Katie. "I…ah… I don't think you should be pushing other kids off their seats, kiddo."

She shrugged. "I know. Mr. Carson is the bus driver and he scolded me. I apologized to Jackie, so we're still friends."

"Oh, well. I'm glad that ended on a happy note."

"Yep. And your cupcake survived."

Mac couldn't stop the chuckle that slipped from his throat. Katie grinned, her glee at her success in bringing it home to him plastered on her little face. He thought he heard Isabelle choke on her own laughter. "When do I get to eat it?" he asked, taking it from her.

"Now."

"Really? I don't have to wait until after dinner?"

"Yep. You're big. You gots lots of room in your tummy, so you can eat it and not spoil your dinner." She frowned. "I wish I was big. But eat it." She hopped on one foot. *"Eat it."*

Mac pulled the paper wrapper away and popped the cupcake in his mouth. Chewed and swallowed. "That was delicious." It really was. "Thank you."

Katie's eyes went huge in her face. "Did ya even taste it?"

Laughter exploded from him. So hard that he lost his balance and went down on his rear. Oh, this precious child. His chuckles threatened to turn to sobs as his own son's little face came to mind. Would he have had such an infectious and happy personality or would he have been more serious like Mac? The fact that he'd never know washed over him, choked him. He had to swallow three more times before he could find his smile again. "Thank you, kiddo, that was really sweet of you."

"Katie," Isabelle called, "why don't you go on inside and wash your hands? Then you can play with Lilly for a bit before we do a little homework, okay?"

"Okay, Izzy-belle. See you later, Mr. Mac." She scampered off.

Mac cleared his throat and scrambled to his feet. "She's a mess," he said.

"She made you think of your son."

He was truly amazed at her powers of observation. "She did."

"Are you all right?"

He shrugged. "I'm better than I was." The smile he shot at her didn't feel nearly as forced as it usually did. "I haven't laughed like that in a while." Since before the accident. The moment of joy had felt...good. Very good.

"Stick around. You might find that happening on a daily basis with Katie."

He nodded. "Guess I'll get back to the fence."

She turned to look at it, then back at him, her eyes soft. His heart did another weird thump. Very different from the one Katie had caused. Mac's gaze roamed her face. He noted that her nose was a little too sharp and one brow was a fraction higher than the other. She also had a faint scar on her chin. But put it together with her high cheekbones and compassionate heart, she was one of the most beautiful women he'd ever met. Inside and out.

"It's looking wonderful," she said. "Thank you."

"Yes, ma'am." Movement over her left shoulder distracted him. "I see the watchdog is here."

She followed his gaze. They both watched the officer take up a position on the porch swing. "Ben's a good man," she said. "I went to high school with him."

"I guess you know just about everyone in Timber Creek?"

"I know a lot of them, for sure, but mostly just the people I went to high school with and their families. Although, the town is growing by leaps and bounds. New people are moving here every day. When I was at the grocery store, the teenager that helped get my groceries to the car was someone I'd never met before. But for the most part, yes, I know most everyone." She shrugged. "That's small-town living for you."

"I'm not sure I'd like that. I'm originally from Atlanta and even the ranch I had was within fifteen minutes driving distance to just about any store you can think of. Seems to me this is too much like being in a fishbowl where everyone knows all your embarrassing moments."

"Hmm. Well, there is that, of course, but everyone also knows your needs and does their best to help out. Like with the Day at the Ranch coming up. I've had donations coming in hand over fist. From vet services to hay, to cupcakes, chicken platters and drinks. I'd say the pros outweigh the cons. Most of the time, anyway."

His lips tugged upward once more. "I'll reserve judgment." He paused. "But if everyone in the town is like you, then I can definitely see why there'd be more pros than cons."

Surprise flickered in her gaze and her features softened, piercing him right in the heart. He liked her. "Thanks," she said. "And I think withholding judgment is a very wise decision until you have all the facts." Her gentle approval made him want to tell her he'd like any town as long as she was a part of it, but he bit his lip and scanned the area, wondering if the man who'd caused so much trouble was out there. And if he was, what did he think about the police cruiser in plain sight?

He hoped it would scare the guy off.

If it didn't, they were in more trouble than they thought. The weight of his weapon in the holster was a comfort that reassured him he was more than capable of making sure Isabelle and the kids stayed safe from harm.

SEVEN

Isabelle rose early the next morning and, once again, enjoyed a short conversation with Mac on the porch before getting the kids off to school.

Now, as she sat in her office preparing for her meeting in town, she let herself ponder the man—and her heart's flip-flopping reaction every time she was in his presence.

She liked him. A lot. She knew herself well enough to label those feelings as attraction. She drew in a deep breath. Okay, so she was attracted to the man and that bothered her. And not because she felt like she was betraying Josiah in any way. She'd loved her husband and he'd loved her. But she knew he'd want her to be happy. To love again. She just didn't expect to be drawn to a man like Mac. He was a drifter, just passing through to earn a little money before he left. Liking him was one thing; letting her heart get involved would be quite another.

He'd been quiet this morning, like he had

some deep thoughts that he was considering sharing, but in the end, he'd chosen not to. She didn't ask him about his family, and he didn't bring it up. "Gonna get back to working on that fence until you're ready to leave," he'd said. She'd watched him leave and then headed to her office.

Isabelle blew out a sigh and pulled up the donations spreadsheet. Running a nonprofit organization meant she relied on the generosity of others to provide a living for herself and those working for her. Of course, she received money from the state for the children—and that was what she used it for. The children.

But things were still pretty tight and didn't leave room for a lot of extras. She could only pray that the Day at the Ranch fundraiser would turn out to be a success like it usually did.

After a phone call from Cheryl, who wanted an update on everything, Isabelle focused on making sure her numbers balanced and contacting those participating in the weekend.

The time went quickly in spite of her multiple trips to check on Lilly, who was under the care of Ms. Sybil. The older woman was much more than just a cook. She was also a good friend and a babysitter when Isabelle needed her. A role she relished, as she'd never had any children of her own. The last time Isabelle stepped into the den, Ben came from the kitchen, two chocolate chip cookies in hand. He stopped when he saw her. "I hope it's okay," he said, holding up the cookies. "Ms. Sybil's rocking Lilly to sleep and she told me to help myself."

"Absolutely."

"There's been no sign of any trouble, but that may mean he's just regrouping."

"I know. Thank you for taking the time to do this."

He ate one cookie much like Mac had downed Katie's cupcake.

"Sure thing." He ate the other cookie and headed for the door. "After you and Mac take off, I'm going to do a quick perimeter check." He held up a key. "I'll lock up behind myself."

"And set the alarm."

"Absolutely. I'll keep the house in view at all times." He hesitated. "I don't mind staying inside, but I feel like I need to be seen outside. Let anyone watching know that we're watching for them, too. Does that make sense?"

"Perfect sense." Although, the thought of someone hiding in the trees watching the house sent shivers of dread all over her. But Ben was here. The other children were at school. Everyone was safe. For now.

She glanced at the clock and gasped. "I've got

to go." She ran out the door to see Mac leaning against his truck.

When he opened the door, she slid into the passenger seat and buckled up. Once he was settled behind the wheel and they were on their way, she shifted so she could see the side mirror. "Thank you for doing this."

"Happy to. I need a few things from the hardware store and this gives me a good chance to pick them up."

"If it's for my place, I have an account there. Feel free to get whatever you need, and just bring me receipts."

"I don't need much for the ranch. I'm just running short on nails. I have a few personal items to grab."

"Okay, of course." She fell silent, feeling like the conversation was going from stilted to awkward. "So—"

"Tell me what got you interested—" Mac said at the same time. He stopped. "Sorry. What were you going to say?" He adjusted the rearview mirror and she noted that he never relaxed his vigilance. It made her feel safe and worried at the same time.

"Nothing. You first."

"I was just going to ask you how you got interested in fostering kids."

"Oh." She took a deep breath. "My husband,

Josiah, and I were married for a little over two years when we decided we were ready to expand our family. We tried for a year and...well, we're not sure why, but we never got pregnant. And no, we didn't do any medical testing to find out why. We intended to, but decided to start the fostering process first. Once that was underway, if we still weren't pregnant, we'd try to find out why. Between the ranch and work and everything involved in the fostering application, we never got around to it. As soon as we were approved, we had our first placement."

"Wow, that was fast."

She let out a low laugh and checked the mirror once more. No one following them. Isabelle let out a relieved breath. "Faster than usual," she said. "We just never ran into any snags in the process, and before we knew it, a young teen who came from a rough background was in our home. She was so defiant and angry. It was then that I got the idea for turning the ranch into a therapeutic experience. Josiah agreed and we got started with it. It took time and a lot of paperwork, but we finally got our nonprofit accreditation and things took off from there. Brianne was a hard case, but she finally softened toward us when she realized we weren't going to kick her out or trade her in for a more well-behaved kid." She shot him a tight smile.

"You're a pretty amazing person, aren't you?"

She laughed. "I don't know about that, but I do believe in doing what we can to make other people's lives better. And if that means being inconvenienced occasionally or helping a traumatized teen through a rough patch that's not their fault, or losing sleep because of a confused baby, then I'm okay with that."

Mac fell silent and she followed his lead, her eyes going to the side mirror, unable to stop looking for the motorcycle.

"He's not going to get whatever he wants, Isabelle, I promise."

She raised a brow at him, surprised he'd read her thoughts so easily. "I appreciate the reassurances, but you can't make that promise. No one can."

"Okay. True." She could tell he didn't like that thought. "But," he said, "I *can* promise to do my best to make sure you and the others stay safe."

His fingers clutched the wheel so tightly his knuckles turned white. She placed a hand over them and squeezed gently. "Thank you." She paused. "Why do you care so much?" At his frown, she paused. "That didn't come out right. I simply meant, you've only just met us and I can tell being our protector means a lot to you. And I think it's more than the former cop talking."

He shot her a quick glance. "I have a real problem when innocent people suffer because someone else makes a bad—or illegal—choice."

"Does that passion stem from losing your wife and child?"

He hesitated, then shrugged. "I don't know. That could be part of it, but I've always been that way. I have a younger sister who liked to get into mischief. I was forever telling her that watching out for her was a full-time job in and of itself. Thankfully, she's married now with three kids—two boys and a girl. Just had the baby girl two months ago."

And she felt quite sure he hadn't gone to see his sister or the new baby. Although he was in a better emotional place than he used to be— at least according to him—his pain still went deep. Isabelle's heart hurt for him. "And your parents?"

"They live about a mile from my sister and relish the grandparent role."

"They all sound lovely."

"They are." He sounded subdued, as though he didn't want to talk about them anymore.

Soon he pulled onto Main Street and she sighed. "Why have I never even noticed motor-cycles before and now I see them everywhere?" Two were parked at the gas station and one in the parking lot of the bank next door.

"I know," he said. His jaw tightened and his gaze scanned the bikes. "None of those are the one that I've seen on your property, but I'll know it when I see it. And when I see it, the owner is going to have a lot to answer for."

Just before they reached the restaurant, Mac's phone buzzed. He didn't recognize the number, but the area code was local. He activated the Bluetooth function. "Hello?"

"This Mac McGee?"

"It is."

"This is Officer Jay Parks. Regina called and asked if we could get together this morning to work on a sketch?"

"That's fine."

"Can you meet me at the station in about an hour?"

"An hour's good." That would give him time to get what he needed from the hardware store first. "See you then." He hung up and turned to Isabelle. "How long do you think you'll be?"

"No more than a couple of hours, but you take your time. I'm not in a hurry. If you're still with the sketch artist, I'll get Regina to drop me at the station."

"Sounds like a plan." Mac let Isabelle out in front of the restaurant's door. "I'll text you when

I finish up. If I'm done before you are, I'll just come and pick you up right here, okay?"

"Sure. Thank you, Mac."

"Of course." He waited until she was inside, then watched through the window as she greeted Regina with a hug before he pulled away from the curb. It didn't take him long to find a parking spot. He got out, his gaze traveling in a circle, looking for the mysterious motorcycle rider—or anyone who sparked his internal alarms.

Nothing and no one stood out to him, and with Isabelle safely in the presence of a police officer, he felt comfortable heading into the hardware store three doors down. The store was situated between a beauty salon and a children's consignment store. Large windows with displays of tools and lawn equipment were tasteful and meant to entice the window-shopper to walk in.

Mac did so, feeling right at home in the place.

While he shopped, the conversation with Isabelle played like a loop in his mind. He hadn't talked to his sister since the birth of his niece. He'd sent a card and some money but hadn't picked up the phone to call and congratulate her on the new addition. And she'd quit calling him after he'd continued to let her calls go to voice mail. Her last call had been a week ago. Shame engulfed him. He couldn't avoid her forever.

But he wasn't aiming for forever, just long enough that it didn't hurt to think about the fact that her baby girl was the same age as Little Mac when he'd died. The familiar pain squeezed his chest and he sighed. The ache would always be there, and he needed to just acknowledge that and stop trying to run from it. But every time he tried, the pain nearly suffocated him. Running had kept him from falling into a pit of depression that nothing could have brought him out of.

His gaze traveled in the direction of the café and his heart lightened slightly at the thought of Isabelle. But maybe, just maybe, he might finally be ready to stop running.

Maybe.

Once he finished grabbing what he needed, he paused at the candy aisle and snagged a bag of lollipops for the kids. He'd seen the older teen, Zeb, give Katie the last sucker to put in her lunch box even though Mac could tell he'd wanted it for himself. Mac hefted the bag. Now they'd have enough to last for a while. He stepped up to the cash register, and a man in his midseventies smiled through his bushy mustache and beard while the overhead light bounced off his bald head. "Howdy. You new around here?" He grabbed the suckers, scanned them and dropped them in the bag.

"I am. Name's Mac McGee I just started working at Isabelle Trent's ranch."

"Isabelle's a great lady. She's much loved in this town. So glad she's got some more help out there. I'm Grady O'Malley. Happy to have you."

"Thanks." Mac glanced behind him, and seeing no one else waiting, leaned forward. "Say, do you know a guy who rides a Yamaha bike with blue trim?"

Grady finished scanning the items and frowned. "Not that I can think of. Lots of bikes around here. They're cheap and easy for a lot of households that only have one income."

"The rider has blue eyes and a goatee. Last I saw him, he had on a black hoodie and jeans."

The man shook his head. "Can't think of anyone matching that description right off the bat. It might come to me later."

"Okay. Thanks."

"Why you asking?"

"I'd like to talk to the owner. Had a little issue that I need to clear up with him and he got away before I got his name."

"Well, lots of folks come through here. I can see right out into the parking lot from here, so if you leave me your number, I'll give you a ring if the fella shows up."

Mac paid for his goods and left his number with Grady. An idea formed and he decided it might be good to make his way to the restaurants and shops, asking the same question and leaving his information.

Surely someone knew the guy with the motorcycle? And while the cops were looking, Mac didn't figure it would hurt to give them a hand in the search.

EIGHT

Isabelle sat across from Regina and Travis, sipping her coffee, thankful for caffeine and friends who were as passionate about her work as she was.

Travis had already promised to come out that afternoon to help the kids practice the little show they would put on next weekend. Pig roping was always the highlight of the event. For the kids and the adults.

Donna Taylor, owner of the best—and only—bakery in town, hurried through the door and slipped into the seat they'd held for her. Her chest heaved and her blue eyes flashed while tendrils of gray hair swirled around her cheeks. "I'm so sorry I'm late," she said. "Ever since I turned sixty, I can't seem to get anywhere on time. You'd think being directly across the street, I'd be able to be punctual. But I had a last-minute order I had to get in the oven because Chelsea wasn't there yet." She stopped and drew in a deep breath. Chelsea Banks, Donna's part-time help. "And then some wild man on a motorcycle almost ran me down."

Isabelle's attention sharpened on the woman. "What? Do you know who the wild man was?"

"No." Donna pursed her lips. "I didn't get a look at his face. He had on one of those helmets with the tinted visor. No idea who he was."

Chills danced across Isabelle's arms and she couldn't help wondering if it was the same person who'd caused all of her trouble. Her gaze collided with Regina's. "When did you first notice this guy?" Regina asked Donna.

"He was staring through the window of the café. I thought he might be waiting on someone to come out, but then he just gunned that thing and nearly took me out while I was in the middle of the crosswalk." She paused. "He had an ugly tattoo of some kind of snake on his right hand. I did notice that."

Regina narrowed her eyes and shot another glance at Isabelle. "Good to know, Donna. I'll keep a watch out for him."

"Well, someone sure should, so thank you." She patted Isabelle's hand. "Anyway, that's why I'm late, my dear."

"It's fine, Donna," Isabelle said. "Travis just got here, too. I'm just thankful that you'd all take the time to come. Why don't you go first so you can get back to the store?"

Donna recounted her donation and asked, "If we have anything left over, I think I'll just box it up and leave it with you. If you want, you can sell the leftovers in bundles as people are leaving and keep the money for the program."

"Oh, that's a wonderful idea," Isabelle said, "and so very sweet. Thank you."

"My pleasure." Donna checked off her list. "I'll just need a couple of people to help serve."

Isabelle nodded. "That's not a problem. I have four returning foster kids who've RSVP'd that they wouldn't miss the weekend for the world. You know them all. The wonderful thing is, they know how everything works and will be a big help. Especially with the kids I have now."

"Then I think we're good to go." Donna stood. "I'll see you this weekend."

After the woman left, Isabelle couldn't help noticing that Regina's gaze followed her until she disappeared, then continued to roam the restaurant. Ever since they'd sat down, Regina was constantly watching the door, the windows, the other occupants. Isabelle knew it was because she felt she needed to be hyperalert to any danger that might present itself, but still... "Relax, Reg," she said, her voice soft.

Regina jerked, then let out a low laugh. "Sorry. Am I that obvious?"

"A bit."

"What's going on?" Travis asked.

Isabelle filled him in and his eyes widened with each word. "You're kidding."

"I wish I was."

"That's awful. Valerie didn't tell me."

"Valerie doesn't know. I haven't said anything to anyone. The last thing I need is bad publicity for next weekend." She paused. "That didn't sound right. I'm really praying that the person causing all the trouble is caught before then. If not, if there's even a hint that anyone could be in danger, then I'll have to cancel and just hope the donors will continue to write their checks to the nonprofit even though they didn't get their annual visit."

Travis shook his head. "Don't tell Valerie. She might just camp out on your doorstep, she'd be so worried."

"I'm not saying anything to anyone right now. Just you and the police and those of us at the ranch know about this. And, of course, Cheryl." Travis knew Cheryl from high school, as well. "I'm obligated to keep her updated."

"And she thinks the kids are safe there?"

"Of course. Ben is there. He's going to practically move in until this person is caught." She told him about Mac, as well.

"Are you sure it's not this Mac person causing the trouble? What do you know about him, anyway?"

Isabelle shot him a gentle smile. "Mac is wonderful. His background check came back clean. He's been a real friend and a big help so far."

Regina nodded. "He's a former cop, too, so that's a bonus."

With a shrug, Travis turned his laptop around to face her. "All right, then. I think we've gone over just about everything and we're ready. What do you think, Isabelle? Are we missing anything?"

"If we are, I don't know what it is," Isabelle said. "I think we're good." She let out a low chuckle. "I don't know why I start to panic this time every year. It all comes together so perfectly when it's all said and done."

Regina patted her hand. "We've got this and so does the Lord."

"Absolutely," Isabelle said. "I know in the end, He's the one in control."

Regina's phone dinged and she glanced at it. A smile curved her lips. "And that's my friend Evie." Regina read silently then looked up. "She's going to bring Cosmo, her patrol dog, and says they'll be happy to do a demonstration."

"That's wonderful," Isabelle said, thrilled. Everyone loved to see a K-9 in action. "Peter will be all over that, won't he, Travis?" Peter, Travis's ten-year-old son, wanted to be a K-9 handler when he grew up. Travis, lost in thought, didn't answer, his gaze on his phone. "Travis?"

He blinked and looked up. "Oh, sorry. What?"

Isabelle frowned. "You okay?"

"Yeah. Sorry. Ah… Valerie called and left a message. I'll call her back in a minute. What'd you say?"

Isabelle repeated herself.

"Should I bring my old football pads and helmet?" Travis asked, his tone dry.

Regina smirked. "I think they'll supply all that. You want me to put you down as the volunteer bad guy?"

He laughed. "I was definitely kidding. I'll pass, thanks."

Isabelle glanced at her watch. Mac should be getting close to being finished. "I need to pick up some allergy medication for Katie, then get on home."

Regina stood. "I'll walk over to the pharmacy with you, then we can go by the station, since Mac hasn't texted yet."

"Great. Thanks."

Travis checked his phone and groaned. "I've got another appointment and I'm going to be late. I need more than one secretary." To Isabelle, he said, "I'll see you and the kids this afternoon."

"Bring Valerie and your kids."

He raised a brow. "Do you really think they'd let me come without them?"

"Very true. See you all later. Now go, you're going to be late."

He bolted for the exit and Regina shook her head. "Donna's got nothing on him. He'll be late to his own funeral."

"You speak truth, my friend. He just books his calendar too full, but he'll be on time this afternoon. Valerie and the kids won't let it be otherwise."

"Agreed." She paused. "Change of subject. I noticed your reaction when Donna was talking about that guy on the motorcycle. Wonder if it's the person who's been attacking you?"

"I have no idea, but it seems like much more than a coincidence to me. Donna said he was watching the café." Isabelle bit her lip and frowned. "Which means he might have been watching me."

"And when he realized you didn't have the baby, he drove off, almost hitting Donna in the process?"

Isabelle drew in a sharp breath. "You think so?"

"I don't have any proof, of course, but I'm leaning in that direction." She pulled out her cell phone. "I'm going to call Ben and update him, then see if there's any security footage we can watch."

"Good."

Two minutes later, Regina nodded and hung up. "Ben's watching the monitor. He said Lilly was sleeping in her crib and Ms. Sybil is asleep in the recliner. He said he's keeping an eye out and is even more alert than ever now, but from his perspective, all is fine at the ranch."

With a slow nod, Isabelle ordered her pulse to slow as she mentally repeated Regina's words. *All is fine at the ranch.* But she couldn't help adding, *For how long?*

Because the motorcycle man wasn't finished with whatever it was he was after.

Mac had just finished up with the sketch artist when his phone buzzed, alerting him to a text message that Isabelle was heading his way with Regina at her side. The station was about two blocks from the café and across the street, so it wouldn't take them long. He shook hands with the artist, grabbed several copies of the printed sketch and headed for the door.

When he stepped outside, a raindrop hit his

cheek and he glanced at the clouds hovering above. He frowned, thinking about Isabelle's friend who was supposed to come out that afternoon to work with the kids. The rain might mess up the plans. He scanned the street, noting the cars parked at the meters and the people at tables under the umbrellas at a popular chain restaurant. Even as he watched, several picked up their food and moved inside.

For some reason, he was antsy, nervous, wanting to look over his shoulder.

When Isabelle appeared around the corner with Regina beside her, he wanted to hurry to her and usher her inside somewhere. Anywhere.

She laughed at something Regina said then turned and caught his eye. Her smile widened and she waved as they stepped off the curb to cross the street.

A car engine revved, the sound capturing his attention. He swiveled his head to see a red Mustang pull from a parking spot and into the lane.

Regina and Isabelle were halfway through the crosswalk when the Mustang sped up. Terror spiked in him. After all that had happened to Isabelle in the last couple of days, he knew exactly how this was going to play out.

"Isabelle! Get back!" She slowed, paused.

"The car!" His cry echoed in his head. As if in slow motion, Mac watched.

The Mustang drew closer. Isabelle spun toward it and Regina grabbed her arm, shoving her away while the car put on a burst of speed. Isabelle stumbled and hit the asphalt just as the vehicle shot past her. Regina fell and rolled. Then was still.

Mac raced toward the women, trying to get a view of the license plate, but more focused on reaching Isabelle and Regina. Isabelle pushed to her knees, her eyes landing on her friend. She cried out and scrambled to Regina's side.

From the corner of his eyes, Mac could see the onlookers gathering. "Someone call 911!"

"Already did," a voice shouted back.

"Isabelle? Regina?" He dropped beside them. Regina groaned and her hand went to her arm.

"The car hit her," Isabelle said, her worried gaze scanning her friend.

"Just a clip," Regina ground out between clenched teeth. "I'll be all right. Please tell me someone got the plate."

A siren sounded not too far away, and Mac looked back over his shoulder to see an ambulance making its way toward them. Isabelle held Regina's hand. "It was a solid clip, Reg," she said, her voice soft, strained with concern.

"Hold on, help's coming." She looked up at Mac. "I'm going to ride with her."

"I'll be right behind you."

"And I'll be behind both of you," Grant said, stepping next to them. He knelt beside Regina as the paramedics pushed their way through.

Mac gripped Isabelle's upper arm and pulled her back. "Come on, let them do their job."

The tremors that shuddered through Isabelle went straight up his arm. He shifted her closer to his side, tucking her under his arm and watching the area around them. The red Mustang was gone, but he'd gotten a partial plate. In a town this small, it was only a matter of time before the cops found it.

While the paramedics worked quickly to get Regina onto the stretcher and into the back of the ambulance, the dark clouds released their bounty. The rain fell fast and hard. Isabelle didn't seem to care; her only thought was for her friend.

Once Regina was in the ambulance, Grant turned to Isabelle and motioned her over. Mac hurried her to the back and she climbed inside.

"I'll see you there," he said. "But whatever you do, don't be alone."

"I won't." The doors shut and Mac bolted for his truck. The ambulance took off and all Mac could do was pray Regina would be okay and protect Isabelle from the guy who'd just tried to kill Isabelle.

NINE

Isabelle followed Regina into the hospital but was told to hang back in the triage area while Regina was rushed to the back. "I'll let you know something soon," a nurse called over her shoulder.

Isabelle pressed her palms to her eyes for a moment and turned to see Mac walking through the entrance. His gaze locked on hers and she sighed when he bolted to her side. "Thank you," she said.

He raised a brow. "For what?"

"For being here. I don't know what I did to deserve having you step into my life, but I thank God that He sent you when He did."

A strange look crossed Mac's face for a brief moment before he blinked it away. "I don't know that God had anything to do with it." His jaw tightened and he looked away. Then back. "To be honest, before my wife and son were killed, I'd never been one to run away from troubles."

He offered her a slight shrug. "I guess old habits die hard in certain situations, because I can't just turn my back on you. Not if I can make a difference and help keep you and those kids safe."

"You're a good man, Mac McGee."

His eyes slid from hers once more and he shook his head. "I think the jury's still out on that one."

The glass doors to the ER swished open and Grant stepped inside, spotted her and Mac, and headed their way. Before she could greet him, the other doors opened and the nurse who'd promised to bring her information on Regina walked toward them. Distracted from Mac's cryptic words and the deputy's presence, she focused on the nurse. "How is she?"

"She's going to be fine. She also gave me permission to update you. It seems the mirror of the car caught her upper arm. The doctor's ordered X-rays to see the extent of the damage. Right now, she's in a bit of pain, so we're working on getting that under control. Then we'll get her back to Radiology for the pictures."

"When can I see her?"

"You can go back now, if you want. It'll be about thirty minutes before we can get the X-rays done."

"Thank you." She turned to Mac. "Can you

please call Cody Ray and Ms. Sybil and let them know what's going on? I'll call Valerie in a bit and tell her today's not a good day for Travis to come out." She pointed to the glass doors. "It's raining, anyway. Maybe tomorrow will work better."

"Sure. I'll take care of it all. Text me Valerie's number and I'll even call and explain things to her."

"I'll do that. Thank you, Mac. A hundred times, thank you." She hugged him. A tight squeeze, then she pulled back to snag her phone from her pocket. Isabelle followed the kind nurse through the doors and into the patient area of the ER. "Room four," the nurse said. "She's on some pain meds, so I'm not sure how coherent she'll be."

"I understand. Thank you." Isabelle slipped into the room and found Regina on the bed, her eyes closed, her pale cheeks almost matching the sheets in color. She shuddered, texted Mac the information she'd promised him, then tucked her phone away. She walked to Regina's bedside and noted they'd splinted her left arm to hold it stable while she waited for the X-ray. "How are you doing?" she asked, taking her friend's good hand in hers.

Regina's eyes flickered open and slowly focused. "Hey," she slurred. "I'm doing okay. I think. Arm feels a bit better."

"Yeah, they've got you on some pretty powerful painkillers." She paused. "I'm so sorry, Reg. You're here because of me and I can't stand it."

"Nope. Here because of the guy who didn't bother to stop while we were in the crosswalk." She took a deep breath and let it out on a long sigh. "They get him?"

"No. Not yet. Mac's out there talking to Grant." She paused. "I think the driver did that on purpose. I think he was aiming for me, Regina."

Her friend's gaze sharpened in spite of the drugs. "Why? Could have been an accident. Maybe he was texting and driving or not paying attention. Something like that."

Could have been. But Isabelle didn't think so. And Regina was in no condition to worry about it. "It's possible. I guess we'll know when we know. Close your eyes and rest. I'll wait here until they come get you for the X-rays."

There was no protest from Regina as her eyes drifted shut. Isabelle's throat tightened and she tried to swallow the sudden lump. "God, please," she whispered, "please watch over everyone. Don't let anyone else get hurt because of me. Show us who's doing this. Please." She ran out of words but rested in the peace that God knew her heart. That He understood the words she couldn't find.

She might not have seen the driver thanks to the tinted windows, but she'd heard the engine start when she'd walked past the car. Like he'd been sitting there, waiting for her? She closed her eyes and thought back to those crazy moments of sheer terror. Yes, the engine had started as she'd stepped past the Mustang. It had waited until she and Regina were at the corner of the intersection.

They'd been chatting, but Isabelle had been watching, listening...aware of her surroundings in a way she'd never been before, thanks to all of the scary incidents.

At the intersection, they'd waited for the light to change and then started across. She'd looked up to see Mac and waved. He'd smiled, waved back, and then his expression had turned to concern, and quickly, horror. She'd heard his cry about the car, heard the revving engine. Knew something was terribly wrong. Then Regina had pushed her backward. She could still feel the fall, the scrape of the asphalt on her palms. The bruise on her hip where she'd landed.

The blast of hot air that had swept over her as the car had zipped past.

Then the sound of the mirror catching Regina's arm.

She shuddered.

But she hadn't seen the driver's face or gotten a plate. She could only hope someone else had done so.

A knock on the door jolted her from her thoughts. Before she could call out, it opened and an orderly entered, pushing a wheelchair. The woman was in her early twenties, with dark eyes that narrowed in sympathy when she saw Regina on the bed. She placed a gentle hand on Regina's shoulder to rouse her. "It's time to make our way back for the X-rays. Do you think you can get into the chair with some help?"

"Guess we'll find out," Regina said. She sat up with a groan. "My head is swimming." She lay back.

The orderly pushed the wheelchair to the side. "Then we'll just take the bed with us."

Isabelle gave Regina a light hug. "I'll be in the waiting room if you need me."

"My mom is on the way," she said. "You need to get home to those kids. They'll be getting out of school soon."

With a glance at her watch, Isabelle swallowed a sigh. Regina was right as usual. "Okay, but you'll call me as soon as you get home? Or at least text me? Or have your mom do it?"

"Of course."

Once Regina was out the door and on her way

to get X-rays, Isabelle returned to the waiting room to find Mac still talking with Grant. They turned to her when she walked up. "I guess you need my statement, as well?" she asked.

He nodded. "Might as well get this done. Why don't you have a seat?"

Isabelle sat and recounted everything she remembered while Grant took notes. When she finished, she looked at Mac. "If you hadn't called out, I don't know that I'd be here right now." She slid her gaze back to Grant. "It was Mac's warning that clued me in something was really wrong. Regina, too."

Mac squeezed her fingers and Isabelle once again sent up silent prayers of thanks to God for bringing Mac into her life. She looked at the clock on the wall. "I need to get going. The kids will be home soon." Ms. Sybil could more than take care of the children, but the simple truth was, Isabelle wanted to be there to hug them and reassure herself that they were safe. And spend some time loving on them.

Everything had been so chaotic lately that while she might have been there physically, she'd been mentally preoccupied. Maybe the rain was a blessing in disguise, slowing the day down and giving her some time with the kids.

Mac escorted her to the door of the hospital. "Wait here. I'll get the truck and pull up."

She nodded and he darted out the door and into the rain.

"Excuse me."

"Oh, so sorry." Isabelle moved to the side of the doorway, realizing she was blocking it.

Minutes ticked past and she finally spotted Mac's truck turning into the circle.

She placed a hand on the door when someone bumped into her. She started to turn, but something pressed into her lower back. "Don't move," the low voice said in her ear. "Don't scream, don't do anything stupid, or I'll shoot you. You have my baby and I want her back."

Mac pulled up in front of the doors to see Isabelle standing right where he'd left her. Only something was wrong. Her wide eyes met his and then she disappeared from view. Like she'd been yanked aside? He slammed the truck in Park and bolted out of the driver's seat to race inside. She was gone. He raced to the information desk, where a woman sat, speaking on the phone. "This is an emergency," he panted. "I need you to put that person on hold, please."

With a frown, she complied. "What is it?"

"Did you see a woman standing at the door?" He described Isabelle. "She would have been watching for me."

"I saw her, but she just walked down that hall-way with a man."

"No," he retorted. "Call Security. See if they can find her. That man's trying to kidnap her." It might be a stretch, but he didn't think so. Isabelle wouldn't have gone with anyone when she knew he'd be right back.

The woman's eyes went wide, but she acted without hesitation and hung up on the person she had on hold. Her fingers were dialing while Mac dashed in the direction she'd pointed. *Hang on, Isabelle, I'm coming.* Where would someone take her? *Think, think!*

The parking garage. He'd want to get her out of the hospital, right? A quick scan of the hall-way sent him scurrying to the stairwell, through the heavy metal door and down the steps to the next level and on down. He followed the signs, running flat out, dodging patients and everything else that got in his way. "Sorry. Sorry." Whoever had snatched Isabelle would be walking slowly so as not to attract attention, but Mac didn't care that people stopped to stare. At the bottom of the steps, he pushed through the door that led to the garage.

To his left, parked illegally, was a white Hyundai Santa Fe. The man held Isabelle by the upper arm and had just opened the door to the driver's side.

Mac reached for the weapon in holster. "Isabelle!"

Her captor jerked and turned toward him. When he did, Isabelle jammed her elbow back into the man's stomach, then spun to send a fist into the side of his head. He stumbled back, let out a low scream, and took off running, leaving Isabelle behind. Mac darted to her side, started to take her into his arms, check to make sure she was okay, but she pushed him away. "I'm fine!" She bolted after the man. "Isabelle! No!"

"He's getting away!" She continued her pursuit of the man who'd tried to kidnap her. Mac followed, his heart thudding heavy in his chest. If the man was armed...

The door behind him crashed open and he spared a quick glance over his shoulder to see security guards burst into the garage. "Hey!" They pounded after them.

Seconds later, Isabelle stopped and bent to place her hands on her knees, gulping in breaths. Mac caught up to her. "Are you insane, chasing after him? What were you planning to do if you caught up to him?"

Her gaze met his and she straightened. "I'm sick and tired of being a victim and I need this to stop." A brief, humorless smile pulled the right side of her lips up. "All I wanted to do was stop him. I knew you were right behind me as well as the security guys. I figured if I managed to catch up to him, one of you could take it from there."

His heart slowed its mad thumping and he drew in a deep breath. "Well, those were some kind of self-defense moves you had going on back there. Nice job."

Her cheeks went scarlet. "I took a class in college. I guess it came back to me in sheer desperation." She ran a hand over her eyes. "Or, most likely, God gave me what I needed." She fell silent when footsteps alerted them to the returning security guards.

They were empty-handed and Mac's frustration levels rose. "Guess he got away."

The taller guy nodded. "He did. What happened?"

"I was waiting at the door to the Emergency Department for Mac to pick me up," Isabelle said. "He was only gone a few minutes, but just as he was pulling into the circle that guy came up and put a gun to my back." She frowned. "Or at least I thought it was a gun." A pause. "Assumed it was a gun since he told me not to scream or make a scene or he'd shoot me."

"Did he say anything else?" the officer asked.

"Yes. He said I had his baby and wanted her back. Then, just as we were about to get in the car, he said something like he could deal with the old people, but I was going to have to get him around the cop. I think he was going to force me to drive him to the farm and maybe use me as a hostage to get Ben or Ms. Sybil to give him the baby." A shiver rippled through her and Mac settled his hand on her shoulder. He wanted to shield her, protect her—comfort her.

The security officer nodded, writing in his little book. When he finished, he snapped it shut. "All right. We're going to take a look at the footage, see if we can get a good look at the guy."

"He didn't have a mask on," Isabelle said, "but he did have that hoodie pulled up."

"We'll give it a try, anyway." He nodded to the SUV. "I already had the plates run. It was stolen."

"I'm shocked," Mac said.

"Yeah, I know. But, we've got fingerprints to run. We'll work with the local police and find this guy before too long."

"Thank you. I sure hope *someone* finds him."

Mac agreed, but silently added, *before it's too late.*

TEN

Once Isabelle got home from the hospital, Grant met them at the ranch, wanting a first-hand account of what had happened in the parking garage. He also brought the sketch artist to help fine-tune Mac's previous description.

When they left, Mac went back to his chores, his gun tucked close. Isabelle sat the children down and had a talk with them about being wary of strangers and watching out for each other. They promised to keep an eye out for men on motorcycles and then they played a game until dinner. Before she knew it, the day was over and it was morning once again.

At the breakfast table, Katie looked up from her cereal. "Is Mr. Travis coming this afternoon, because I need to practice my ropin'." She spooned a bite into her mouth and milk dribbled down her little chin.

Isabelle did her best to keep a straight face

while she mopped up the milk. "Yes, ma'am. He should be here when you get off the bus."

"Oh, goody."

This time Isabelle did laugh. Then she glanced over at Lilly in the carrier, her rattle clutched in her tiny fist.

Happy. Content. Adjusted.

And the target of a father who didn't mind using violence against others to get what he wanted. As the day passed, her tension escalated in spite of the police presence and Mac's diligent attention to her and the others. She knew he was watching the trees and the surrounding area as carefully as she was, because his tension was as thick as the summertime humidity in the south.

The hours ticked by with her jumping at every sound and refusing to let the baby out of her sight.

"Isabelle, you're going to give yourself an ulcer," Ms. Sybil said. "Give me the baby and take a break."

Reluctantly, she handed Lilly to the cook and returned to the window. When Valerie's car finally pulled to the top of the drive, she let out a low breath and went out to greet her while Ms. Sybil changed the baby's diaper. Ben had been informed of the pending arrival of the guests, but he stayed on the porch, watching.

She noticed Mac had moved to a section of the fence where he could see what was going on, as well.

Valerie's children tumbled from the back seat. "Hi, Isabelle," Crystal, aged eight, cried out, making a beeline for the house. "I'm going to say hey to the baby."

Isabelle laughed. "All right. Her name is Lilly."

Crystal's older brother, Peter, followed.

Valerie slipped out of the driver's seat with a groan and a low laugh. "How do they have so much energy even after spending all day at school?"

"It's not fair at all, is it?"

"I think I'm going to request that they have them run laps around the school ten minutes before the end-of-day bell rings."

"There's a thought," Isabelle said with a small laugh.

"I have something for you."

"What?"

"Apples on the passenger seat." She walked around to retrieve them and passed them to Isabelle. "The kids pulled these off the tree this morning before school."

"Oh, thank you. We'll have these with our dinner tonight—if Ms. Sybil doesn't decide to make a pie out of them." Isabelle carried the fruit into the kitchen and set the basket on the counter. Valerie followed.

"So, what was the surprise Travis got you?"

Valerie grimaced and he eyes darkened. "A car."

"What? Seriously? And you're not driving it?"

"Ah, no. I told him I didn't want it and to take it back."

"Valerie!"

She shrugged and her eyes slid away. Isabelle noticed the strain on her friend's face and cupped a hand around her upper arm. "Are you okay?"

"I'm fine. Let's focus on something else."

While Danny and Zeb sat at one end of the long table with a board game, Ms. Sybil sat at the other, holding Lilly. Crystal had already started a peekaboo game. The baby's laughter soothed Isabelle's worried heart.

"Where's Travis?" Isabelle asked. She turned to the sink to wash the apples in case someone decided they needed a snack.

"Right behind us. He had a last-minute showing that he didn't want to rush, so I drove separately. And he said he had to stop at a store to pick something up."

"Oh, okay."

"I asked if he couldn't do that on the way

home and he said he had to take care of it now. Honestly, I have no idea what that man's up to lately." Her lips tightened. "Except spending money we don't have. That one's not too hard to figure out."

"Oh, no. Surely not."

Valerie sighed and waved a hand. "Ignore me. I'm in a mood—and aggravated that Travis can't get anywhere except to a showing or a closing on time. Family can always wait, I guess." She checked her phone. "He texted just a minute ago and said he's almost here."

"Wonderful. The kids are so excited."

"Travis is, too. He's like a kid himself some days." She smiled, but Isabelle thought it was a bit stiff.

"Valerie? Is everything okay with you and Travis?" she asked, keeping her voice low while she washed the apples.

Valerie waved a hand. "Yes, fine. Things have been a bit tense since we went so long without a sale, but as of today we've got three showings coming up, so hopefully Travis will be able to relax some. Being here today with the kids will help."

"I'm sorry," Isabelle said. "I didn't realize things were that hard."

"It's okay. It's not like we're going around advertising it. With the closing last week and another possible big sale in the works, he was a little more upbeat today."

"What kind of sale?"

"No idea. He said he didn't want to say too much or get anyone's hopes up in case it fell through."

"I guess that's understandable."

Valerie took the last apple from Isabelle, dried it off and set it with the others back in the basket.

Peter grabbed it from the basket. "Ms. Isabelle, can we see the horses?"

Travis stepped inside the kitchen in time to hear his son's request. "We'll see them, but for now, I've got everything set up outside to practice some roping. Who's interested?"

A cheer went up from Katie and she darted for the door. "I'm first!"

Within seconds, the kitchen was empty of all children except Lilly. Valerie laughed. "I'm going to go watch." She stepped outside to follow her husband and the kids.

Isabelle turned to Sybil. "Whew."

"Ditto." The woman stood. "Do you think it's safe to take this one out?"

Isabelle hesitated. "I don't think so. With all of the kids here and the added protection, it's unlikely someone will try anything, but I'd rather keep her inside."

"Of course. I'll entertain her in her room if you want to go watch the others."

"Thank you. I'll do that for a bit, then come take over and you can go."

"Perfect." Sybil kissed the infant's head and walked out of the kitchen.

Isabelle drew in a deep breath—what felt like the first one she'd had time to take all day. After a glance out the window to see the children having fun and Ben and Mac standing guard around the perimeter, she turned the basket of apples and unloaded them into a basket she pulled from the cabinet.

At the bottom was a note from Valerie.

"Isabelle, thank you so much for your friendship and all you do for the children in this town. I'm blessed to call you my friend."

A lump formed in Isabelle's throat, but she choked it down. She was the one who was blessed. Sure, she'd had some hard times just like anyone else who lived life, but for the most part, she was very, very blessed. She paused, a memory flickering at the edges of her mind.

"Everything okay in here?"

Mac's voice made her jump and exhale. "Yes. Fine." What was it about the note?

"Zoe," she whispered.

"What?"

She looked up, her pulse thrumming. "Valerie

wrote me a sweet note. She does it for people in the town every so often. Her kids' teachers, her pastor, her clients who purchase homes from her and Travis. It's one of the many things that make the townspeople love her."

"And?"

"And," she said, walking toward her room, "every so often I hear from a former foster child. Zoe wrote me a note shortly after she left."

"Zoe?"

"The second foster child Josiah and I took in," she called over her shoulder. "Hold on. I'll explain in just a second." She went to her closet and grabbed a box from the top shelf. When she returned to the living area, Mac was waiting by the window, watching the events going on outside. He turned.

She set the box on the coffee table and opened it. "I know I kept it." She rummaged through the box, looking. And finally pulled a manila folder from the bottom. She opened it and scanned the contents until she spotted what she was looking for. "This. Zoe's letter. I got it about six months after she left, but it wasn't until I saw Valerie's note that it dawned on me the handwriting on the note left in the baby carrier was familiar for a reason." She opened it and read, "'Dear Isabelle, thank you for everything you and Josiah did for me. If not for you, I'd never be where I am now. College. Can you believe it? Anyway, I hope you and Josiah are doing well. You mean the world to me and are a wonderful example of what a mother should be. Sacrificing, compassionate, and mostly, offering unconditional love. Most important, thank you for saving my life and teaching me what a relationship based on love and respect is supposed to look like. You've blessed me in more ways than I'll ever be able to count. Love, Zoe.'"

She fought the tears the note brought to the surface, carefully refolded it and looked at Mac. "Zoe is Lilly's mother."

Mac nodded, his admiration for Isabelle increasing by the moment. "That's an incredible expression of love right there."

"Yes."

Her voice was low. A husky whisper that tightened his own throat. "My wife was like that. She loved everyone, including me, with a passion that I've not seen in many people."

"It sounds so trite to say this," she said, reaching out to curl her fingers around his, "but I really am so very sorry for your loss."

He squeezed her hand. "Thank you." He cleared his throat. "I can say the same for you." They fell silent for a moment. Then Mac said,

"I'll be honest. The pain of losing her has lessened with time, but losing Little Mac…" He shook his head, not sure he could voice his thoughts. "Losing a spouse is one thing." His gaze flicked to hers. "You know how that feels. But losing a child…" He swallowed before he could go on. "You know, when you become a cop, there's the knowledge that every day might be your last. You accept that, make peace with it and move on. At least most cops do. Doesn't mean you're not hyperalert and watching over your shoulder more than the average person, but you live with it. Your family learns to live with it—again, most of the time." He drew in a shuddering breath. "At no point did I expect to lose Jeanie and my son. It came out of nowhere and knocked me so sideways I wasn't sure I'd ever recover."

"Has being a nomad helped you?"

A short, humorless laugh escaped. "Hmm. Yes, in some ways. In other ways, I know I'm just running."

"Well…that's very…insightful of you. Impressively self-aware."

"I've had a lot of time to think."

"Do you think you'll ever settle down? Find a place to call home again?"

Mac studied her for a moment. His mind went to the little place in the valley of the mountains of Virginia. Somehow, he couldn't picture it as vividly as he could just a few days ago. Now the image was blurred, with Isabelle's place superimposed over it. What would it be like to call this place home? With her? He blinked. "Maybe. At some point. It gets easier to think about doing that with each passing day." Especially since he'd arrived at her ranch.

"Good, I'm glad." She hesitated before glancing at the note again. "I guess I should call Grant so he can start looking for whoever the father is. I'm also going to try to get ahold of Zoe. I have an old cell phone number for her, just not sure if it still works."

"Can't hurt to try. While you do that, I'm going to get the golf cart and take a ride around the property. I'll probably be back by the time Grant gets here."

"Okay."

He left her sitting there with the note and her phone pressed to her ear. His tumbling emotions left him reeling. And thinking. He'd had a good marriage, albeit a short one. So had Isabelle, from all appearances. The difference between them was that she hadn't let her husband's death stop her from living—or making an impact on the lives of others.

Shame burned a path from his heart to his cheeks. Had he been so self-absorbed that he'd stopped caring? Stopped seeing the needs of others? Stopped…everything?

Unwilling to examine those questions further, he watched the kids and Travis for a few more minutes. Cody Ray and the dogs had joined them and they didn't seem to be tiring of the games anytime soon. Danny seemed to be having a bit of trouble getting the lasso to work for him and Travis was helping Katie, so Mac walked over to the boy. "Want some help?"

"Sure." Danny passed him the rope.

"So, first of all, you want to make sure your wrist is nice and loose." He demonstrated and Danny copied him. Travis had brought three practice bulls and Mac lined Danny up to face the one in front of him. "Then you twirl the rope like so, holding the longer piece with your other hand. Then you whirl it over your head, aim it, then let it go." Mac released the rope and it settled right over the plastic horns.

"Way to go," Danny crowed.

"Nice job," Travis said.

"Thanks." Mac pulled the rope back in and handed it to Danny. "You keep practicing. I'm going to ride around for a bit, okay?"

"Sure." Danny busied himself with the rope and Mac waved to Ben, hopped in the golf cart and started his perimeter check.

As he rode, he decided one thing he was going

to suggest was an updated security system. If Isabelle was willing—and able—to shell out the money for the purchase of the equipment, he could install it, saving her the labor cost.

His phone buzzed and he glanced at the screen.

His sister. His finger hovered over the swipe button, then switched to the red end icon and tapped it. She'd leave a message if it was something important.

Like she'd done for the birth of his niece. More shame gathered and he sighed, flexed his fingers on the wheel and pulled his mind from his issues. He needed to focus on keeping Isabelle and the children safe. Then, he'd man up and address his personal life. Until then, she and the kids were the priority.

With that settled in his mind, he spun the golf cart to the back of the property and slowly made his way around it, taking notes on vulnerable security spots. He'd mention those to Isabelle after everyone was gone. Just as he pulled back around to the front, Grant's cruiser came into sight. The man parked to the side of the house and Mac guided the golf cart in the space beside him.

Grant stepped out of the car and Mac noted the man's confident stance, the sharpness in his eyes. Mac knew the type. A good cop that made others feel either reassured by his presence or sorry they messed with him. Mac was glad Isabelle had Grant, Ben and Regina on her side.

"You didn't have to drive out here," Mac said.

"I was on my way home, anyway. Thought I'd stop in and check in with everyone. Didn't realize you'd have a crowd." His gaze was on the children in the field. Katie had the rope and was twirling it above her head. It dropped around her, midspin, and she let out a shriek. Grant laughed. "That kid cracks me up."

"You're not alone. They're practicing for the Day at the Ranch festival."

"Right. I'm looking forward to it. I don't need to practice for my bit, though."

"What's your role?"

"Dunking booth stooge." His lips twisted into a rueful smile. "Each year, I say I'm retiring, and each year, I keep coming back."

Mac laughed. "Come on, I think I saw Isabelle walk over to watch all the fun." He sobered. "Any progress on finding our motorcycle-riding attacker?"

Grant's eyes clouded. "None at the moment. I'm hoping Isabelle's going to give me something solid to go on. How's her head where the hammer hit her?"

"Seems to be fine. It's certainly not slowing her down."

"No, it wouldn't."

The two men walked out to the pasture where Travis was working with Danny on roping the horns of a plastic bull. Isabelle stood outside the fence, watching. When she saw them, she strolled toward them, hands in her pockets, uncaring that her boots were covered in mud or that she had a streak of it on her cheek.

Mac reached up without thinking, to brush it away. Her eyes widened and he dropped his hand. "Sorry. You had mud there."

A smile curved her lips. "With all the rain, the pasture hasn't quite dried out yet. When Katie ran over to give me a hug, she passed on some of her mud, too."

Mac cleared his throat and held her gaze a moment longer before she turned to Grant. "The girl's name is Zoe Hawthorne," Isabelle said. She handed him the note Mac recognized as the one she'd kept in her box. "You can use that to compare the handwriting, but I really don't have any doubts that it's her."

"You know where she is?"

"She texted last Christmas and said she was in school at UNC Chapel Hill. Said she got a scholarship and was majoring in education. She also said she was seeing someone, but when I pressed her for more details, she was pretty vague."

"She mention the guy's name?"

"No." She waved her phone at him. "I even scrolled back through the texts to see if she did. But she didn't."

Grant tucked the note into the front pocket of his shirt and nodded. "Should be easy enough to track her down."

"How's Regina?"

"She's home. Her mother's staying with her. Said she's sore, but very grateful things weren't worse."

"Yes, me, too," Isabelle said, her voice low.

A shrill scream pierced the air and the three turned as one. Mac drew in a horrified breath. Katie had wandered farther into the pasture and was now face-to-face with a very angry bull.

ELEVEN

Isabelle didn't stop to think. She raced for the fence, her legs pumping, heart beating like a wild thing in her chest. "Katie! Don't move!"

"Isabelle! Stop!"

Mac's cry pierced her, but she kept going, angling around to the side of the fence so Duke couldn't see her quick actions.

The dogs barked, and she thought she heard Cody Ray tell the boys to hold them. That was one thing she didn't have to worry about. The dogs might distract the bull—or cause him to charge in the blink of an eye.

Duke let out a bellow and horned the ground. Katie stood frozen. Isabelle wasn't sure if it was because the child had heard her order or if she was just so terrified she *couldn't* move. "Please, Lord, please protect that baby. Don't let him hurt her." She whispered the words as she bolted past Danny and Zeb, both of whom looked horrified, and past Travis, Valerie and their children. Isabelle hit the fence and launched herself over just behind the bull's right shoulder. She reached down and scooped up a rock that fit snuggly in the palm of her hand.

"Isabelle…"

Cody Ray's low warning reverberated through her. She heard it, processed it…and ignored it. She'd promised Katie the day she'd arrived, scared and spooked at the slightest sound, that she would take care of her. Even if that meant getting between an agitated bull and the little girl.

Isabelle heard Mac and Grant behind her. "Don't move fast," Isabelle whispered to the terrified five-year-old. "Just back up slowly." Duke swung his attention from Katie to her, then back to Katie. The child didn't budge, but Isabelle could see the tremors racing through her small body. "Katie? Katie, I'm here. Listen to me. Look at me, baby." She kept her voice soft, soothing, calm. Duke snorted and shook his head, pawing the ground. Then he released another loud bellow that echoed through the air. "Katie? Can you hear me? Don't look at Duke, look at me."

Katie's gaze jerked to hers. "That's it, honey, look at me." Isabelle moved slowly around the animal, keeping her distance, while the bull seemed distracted for the moment, his attention swinging back and forth from Isabelle at his side to Katie in front of him.

"Isabelle?" Mac's voice came too close, but he was still on the other side of the fence. She shot a quick glance at him while her heart continued its thunderous beat. Mac climbed over the fence and his feet landed silently on the ground behind her.

"I've got this, Mac." Truly, she didn't know if she did or not. "Katie, walk backward. Very slowly. The policeman's waiting. Don't turn and don't run until I tell you to. If you do what I say, you'll be fine." *Please, God, let her be fine. Don't let Duke charge.*

To Isabelle's relief, Katie took one shaky step back. Then another. And another.

The movement seemed to annoy the bull again. He bellowed once more and stepped forward. Katie froze. Duke lowered his head. Isabelle launched the rock in her left hand, and it hit the bull in his hindquarters. He roared and spun, his focus solely on Isabelle now.

"Go, Katie," Isabelle cried. "Run to Grant!"

The child obeyed and the moment she was within reach, Grant snagged her arm and pulled her behind him. "Run for the fence, Katie," he said. "Go!" He followed her, keeping his body between the animal and the little girl.

Katie's little legs churned. The bull hesitated,

once again seemingly undecided about what bothered him more. He swung back toward Katie, let out another angry bawl, then whipped his attention toward Isabelle. He snorted and roared his displeasure, then blew and stomped at the ground.

Isabelle shot a glance over her shoulder and saw Mac had moved farther into the field to her left. On the other side of the fence, with the others safely behind him, Grant had his pistol out and aimed at the bull.

"Don't shoot him, Grant," Isabelle said. "That little bullet won't stop him. It'll just make him angrier."

"It'll stop him if I get him right between the eyes."

But his angle was off and they both knew he'd never hit the animal in the kill spot. And he most likely didn't have time to move to a place that would afford him the right view. Mac shifted and Duke swung his head toward him, then back to Isabelle.

What was Mac doing? She didn't dare take her eyes from the bull to find out. The huge animal now faced her, like he'd done with Katie a few short seconds ago.

Duke started forward, his razor-sharp horns glinting in the sunlight. Isabelle kept a tight grip on her fear and followed her own advice.

She started walking backward, never taking her gaze from the animal's. He lowered his head, snorted…and charged.

"Isabelle!"

Mac's shout floated over her head.

Isabelle didn't run. She stayed put, shaking, trembling and watching. Waiting for the right moment as each stretch of Duke's legs brought him closer.

As soon as Duke was close enough that she could almost feel his breath on her face, she spun to the side and he roared past. Isabelle sprinted for the closest section of the fence. Panic clenched at her throat. It was too far. She'd never make it.

"Isabelle, run!" Zeb's holler echoed around her. Duke barreled toward her, snorting and blowing. She churned her legs faster…lost her footing and fell. She slammed into the ground and the breath left her. Pain rattled through her, stunning her motionless.

The ground shook, Duke's hooves grew closer. There was no way to outrun the best, so she froze and shut her eyes. "Please, God, rescue me."

And then a thunderous boom crashed through the air. She dared open her eyes and saw Mac standing in the field behind Duke, who lay on his side kicking his feet. A rope was around one of his legs, pulled tight. Mac had managed to maneuver himself behind the bull, lassoed one of his legs and yanked him down. "Run, Isabelle! Get up and run!"

He didn't have to tell her twice. Isabelle rolled to her feet and dashed to climb over the fence. Danny threw himself into her arms, squeezing her around the waist. She looked up to see everyone's eyes on her. "I'm okay, y'all." She forced a smile. "That little ole bull wasn't going to hurt anyone."

Katie burst into tears and Isabelle kept one arm around Danny's shoulders while she held out the other to Katie. The little girl ran toward her...then right past her to fling herself at Mac, who'd jumped the fence while Duke still struggled to get to his feet. Mac caught the child and swung her up into his arms. Katie buried her face in his neck. "You saved her, Mr. Mac. You saved Izzy-belle," she cried through her sobs.

Travis ran toward them, pale and sweating. "Isabelle, are you all right?"

"Yes. I'm okay. Truly." Maybe if she said it enough, she'd start to believe it.

Valerie hugged her and Isabelle held on to her composure by a thread. Now that the danger was over, she needed a good cry. But first...

She hugged each of the older children and even the dogs joined in, prancing around her.

She scratched their ears then went to Katie, who still had her arms around Mac's neck. Isabelle rubbed the little girl's back. "You're okay, Katie. And so am I. God was watching out for us and so was Mr. Mac."

Katie lifted her head from Mac's shoulder and held her arms out for Isabelle, who gathered her close. When she inhaled Katie's sweet, sweaty scent—a combination of baby shampoo and dirt—she nearly broke down. "You're okay, precious girl," she said again.

"I know," Katie mumbled, "but I was scared. Duke's mean."

"Yeah, he is. That's why I sold him to Mr. Galloway. He's already sent me that money and is coming to get him tomorrow."

"Good." Her brow furrowed. "Do you think Duke's sick?"

Isabelle frowned. "I don't know. Why?"

"Cuz when Zeb had that cold, he was kinda like Duke. Grumpy and always blowing his nose. Maybe Duke has a cold."

Mac let out a low chuckle and Isabelle bit her lip on a smile. "Maybe," Isabelle said, her voice soft. "And if he does, he can get better in his new home."

"Okay. Can I have a lollipop? I need one after that."

This time Isabelle did laugh and the urge to

puddle to the ground in tears faded. For the moment. "Sure. Go on inside and tell Ms. Sybil you can have one."

Katie took off and the other kids followed. Travis caught Isabelle's upper arm in a loose grip. "Are you really okay?"

"I'll be sore tomorrow after that fall, but maybe all the ibuprofen I'm taking for the other bumps and bruises will kick in for the new aches and pains." She turned to see Mac watching and she offered him a small, shaky smile. "Thank you."

"You're welcome. I'm just glad my roping days came back to me."

"It was a perfect throw," Travis said with a tight smile. "Maybe you should be the one teaching the kids."

"Nope," Mac said, his expression never wavering from his usual quiet confidence. "I've got a ranch to keep working on. You're a good teacher and they were having a blast with you. You just keep doing what you're doing."

Travis's forced smile relaxed and he nodded. "Appreciate that."

"Sure thing." Mac turned to Ben. "You mind keeping an eye on things?"

"Of course not."

"Thanks." He motioned to Isabelle and Grant. "Can the three of us take a little walk?"

Grant frowned but nodded.

Isabelle shrugged. "Where are we going?"

"Exploring."

"That wasn't an accident," he said as soon as they were out of earshot of everyone. Cody Ray was taking care of the bull and Mac needed some answers. Grant seemed fine to let him lead the way, so he followed the fence toward the back pasture where Duke had been kept.

"What do you mean?" Isabelle asked. "Of course, it was an accident."

"Isabelle, I've been over every acre and inspected every inch of fencing. There's no way that bull got out without some help."

She paled, but her jaw hardened. "All right. Then let's figure out what happened."

Mac's admiration grew. She was a woman used to handling things on her own but wasn't afraid to ask for help when she needed it. His heart reached for her and his mind stepped back. She deserved someone who was going to stick around, someone who wanted the same things in life that she wanted.

Which was…what? Was he making assumptions he shouldn't make?

Grant's phone rang and he snagged it from his pocket. After a glance at the screen, he sighed. "I need to take this. I'm right behind you, though."

He followed at a distance while Mac led the way. As they walked toward the back fence, he glanced at her from the corner of his eye. "So do you see yourself doing this—fostering and running the ranch—for a short time or is this what you see yourself doing the rest of your life?"

She blew out a low breath. "Funny you should ask that now. I was just thinking about that very thing a few weeks ago." She shrugged. "Right now, I know I'm doing what I'm supposed to be doing. It's a calling, I guess. Since Josiah's been gone, it's been hard. So very hard."

"Have you been tempted to quit? Sell? Go back into private practice and see patients?"

"Of course."

"But you don't."

A sigh slipped from her and she turned to wave a hand as though to encompass her property. "This was gifted to Josiah and me by my parents when we got married. They knew our dream was to use it to help people. When we were first married, we weren't exactly sure what we were going to do, just that it would benefit others." She hesitated. "But that was *our* dream. I'm not sure it's still mine." She bit her lip and looked back at him. "Is that awful?"

"No. Not one bit. Things change. Life—and death—changes things. Often before we're ready."

"Yeah."

Grant caught up with them. "That was Regina. She's already begging to come back to work."

Isabelle frowned. "Why's she calling you? Creed's the one to make that decision, isn't he?" Mac thought he remembered Creed being the name of the sheriff.

"Yep, but she was calling me to see if I could talk to Creed and get him to change his mind."

"I hope you told her no."

"I told her she'd take the required days off and then ride a desk until she had clearance from her doctor to do otherwise—just like Creed said."

A small smile played around Isabelle's lips at that statement. "I'm sure she let you know that wasn't acceptable."

Grant rolled his eyes. "It's like you know her well or something."

They crested the next hill and Mac nodded to the fence. "You see what I see?"

"The fence is broken."

They walked over to the boards on the ground. "I guess he did break through it after all," Mac muttered. He strode closer, pulled his work gloves from the back pocket of his jeans and slid his hands into them. He picked up the nearest board. "It's definitely broken due to impact." He pointed at the jagged edges. "Here and here."

"Maybe Duke heard the commotion in the other pasture and decided he didn't like it," Isabelle said.

"It's possible, I suppose." One by one, he examined each piece. And stopped at one of the larger boards. He held it up to her and Grant and pointed to smudges. "What does that look like to you?"

"Dirt?" Isabelle asked.

"Look closer."

She narrowed her gaze, then gasped. "Dirt in the pattern of the bottom of a shoe?"

Grant raked a hand over his chin. "Duke followed the noise in the pasture, but he didn't bust this fence down."

Isabelle pressed a hand to the side of her head like it hurt. "No, he didn't. Someone kicked it down."

TWELVE

Isabelle couldn't get the image of the broken fence board from her mind. That and the memory of Katie in the path of the angry bull. She shuddered and prayed that someday the mental pictures would fade. When she, Mac and Grant returned to the house, Grant took the board to his car, saying he'd have it processed by the crime scene lab in Asheville. He stated he was going to drive it there himself. Once he was gone, she and Mac stepped inside the kitchen to find the kids sitting around the table eating apples. Valerie was gathering her two children to leave. She looked up. "Everything okay?"

"Not really," Isabelle said, "but I'll explain later."

Valerie frowned. "Okay."

"Did you happen to see what Cody Ray did with Duke?"

"He and Ben and Travis got him loaded up

on the trailer. Cody Ray said he was going to deliver him to his new owner a bit early."

"Good." Isabelle had been thinking along those lines, anyway.

Once Valerie, Travis and the children were gone, she left Ben and Mac discussing the best way to upgrade the security system, to step outside for a moment to catch her breath. Her fingers curled around the porch railing and she closed her eyes. "Lord, I don't know what Lilly's father hoped to achieve with that stunt with the bull, but I thank You for keeping everyone safe."

For a long time she stood there, gazing out over the land. The fact that it was hers free and clear never failed to awe her. Gratitude for her parents washed over her and she pulled out her phone. She hadn't spoken to her mom or dad in what felt like forever. Her father had been so busy taking care of her mother and Isabelle had been so involved with everything happening on her end, they hadn't spoken since before Mac had arrived. Of course, her mother's sister was there, so they weren't having to rely on Isabelle for help.

Hi, Dad, she texted. How's Mom? You need anything? Groceries? A break? Love you.

She held on to the phone and rubbed her forehead with her left hand. A headache had started to form behind her eyes. Stress? Definitely.

A car pulled in the drive and she narrowed her eyes, tension threading through her until she recognized the sheriff's vehicle. Sheriff Creed Payne and Isabelle had once been good friends. He'd been two years ahead of her in high school, but their parents were close.

Creed pulled the SUV to a stop and climbed out. "Hey, Isabelle."

"Hey, yourself. What brings you out here?"

He raised a brow. "You have to ask?"

"I guess you got an earful from Grant and Ben?"

"I did."

"Well, as of the moment, all is well." She paused. "I hear you talked to Regina today."

"She's delusional. She needs to heal. End of discussion."

He stepped up beside her just as Mac opened the storm door and walked out onto the porch. "Oh, sorry. Am I interrupting?"

"Not at all," Isabelle said. She made the introductions and motioned for Mac to join her. He mimicked her posture and leaned against the railing.

"Hear you're a former cop," Creed said.

"I am."

"Grant said you've been doing a good job with security out here. Thanks for watching out for Isabelle and the others."

"Of course."

Isabelle's gaze jumped back and forth between the two men. They seemed to be sizing each other up while having a silent conversation that she wasn't privy to. She cleared her throat. "Everything is fine now, Creed. You didn't have to come all the way out here."

"It's not that far. I saw your dad in town yesterday and promised him I'd check in on you." He narrowed his eyes. "You haven't told him about the trouble you're having, have you?"

"No." She straightened and jutted her chin toward him. "And you'd better not tell him, either. He's got enough to worry about without adding me to the list."

Creed hesitated. "Fine. I don't guess he needs to know. I think we're pretty close to catching the person that's causing you all this trouble, anyway."

"Really? Why?"

"I tracked down that former foster kid of yours. Zoe Hawthorne."

"And?"

"She's been in a rehab facility in Asheville."

The air left Isabelle's lungs. "What? But she never had a problem when she was here. Rehab for what?"

"I talked to her college roommate. Apparently, she started dating a guy named Drew

Baldwin. He was bad news and Zoe was easily influenced. He got her involved with drugs and alcohol. When she found out she was pregnant, she got clean. The roommate said she went cold turkey. After Zoe had the baby, this fellow, Drew, kept coming around and making trouble. Knocked Zoe around a bit and threatened to take the baby. In an effort to keep him happy, she resumed that lifestyle and got hooked again."

"Oh, no," Isabelle whispered. She placed a hand over her heart. "I need to go see her."

"You can't. She's not allowed visitors."

"Then how did the baby wind up here?"

"Fortunately, my badge allowed me access to her. I asked her about what her roommate told me, and she broke down. She said Drew would never leave her alone and she was afraid he'd hurt the baby, so she snuck away from the facility one night, caught a bus to Boone, then a taxi to Isabelle's place. Drew had followed on his motorcycle, but Zoe didn't realize it."

"And Drew didn't try to stop her?"

"No, he probably thought he'd see where she was going first. He also probably thought he'd have the opportunity to grab the baby at some point."

"And he would have if I hadn't stepped out of the house when I did," Isabelle murmured.

"And that really made him mad. He left here and went looking for Zoe. He knew she was in the rehab facility and caught her sneaking back in. Drew beat her up when she refused to come back with him and get the baby. She passed out and woke up in the hospital several days later. Thankfully, she was released this morning and is already back at the rehab facility."

Isabelle shook her head. "That poor girl. Why didn't she ask me for help?"

"She did," Mac said, "in a way. She entrusted her daughter to you."

He had a point.

"Okay," Isabelle said. "Now you just have to find Drew, right?"

"We're looking for him as we speak," Creed said. "I checked the two hotels in town and no one by that name's rented a room. I took his driver's license picture by and no one recognized him." Creed flicked a glance at Mac. "Nice job on the sketch, by the way. It was pretty similar to the license picture."

Mac nodded and Creed said, "Anyway, Drew's hiding out around here somewhere." He paused. "Zoe met him at school and said he didn't have family here, so she's not sure who he would stay with or where."

"Could be camping out in the woods somewhere," Mac said.

"I'm guessing that's the case. I've taken his picture into town to the places he might show up to get supplies." He shot Mac a look. "Heard you'd already done that with the sketch."

"I did. But now that there's a name to go with an actual picture of him, maybe someone will spot him."

Creed nodded. "All right, I'll get out of your hair. I just wanted to come by and let you know what was going on with Zoe. Ben and Grant are going to be watching your place closely until this guy is caught."

"What about everything else going on in town?" Isabelle asked. "It's not like you have an unlimited supply of deputies. Don't you need police presence in town?"

"What do you think I'm here for? And if I need some backup, I have a radio to call for help." He smiled. "And this is Timber Creek. Not a whole lot happens here."

"Except my ranch."

"Which is why I've got my deputies out here."

Isabelle winced. "You're going to be working overtime, aren't you?"

"Whatever it takes," Creed said, his eyes serious. "This guy is dangerous and we need him off the street."

"I'll second that," Mac said. "Not just off the street, but behind bars."

* * *

After the sheriff left, Ben followed him so he could get some rest, and Grant stayed to patrol the grounds with Mac, Cody Ray and the dogs. Darkness was falling and Mac wanted to be sure Drew Baldwin wasn't on the property— or at least anywhere near the house.

Finally satisfied, Mac bade Cody Ray and Grant good-night and made his way back to his apartment.

"I don't want to go to bed! I'm not going to go to bed, and you can't make me go to *bed*!"

Mac blinked at the furious emotion beneath the words and detoured from his entrance to the main front door. He rapped on the wood as sobs reached him. The blinds parted, then Isabelle opened the door, a fussy baby in her arms and a weeping Katie clinging to her leg. "Sorry, are we bothering you?"

"Bothering me? Not at all. I came to see if you could use some help."

"There's no way I'm turning that down." She passed him the baby, then swept Katie up into her arms. "If you can get that one to sleep, you'll have an extra star in your crown."

Katie's sobs hiccupped into shuddering breaths. "What's going on with you, Katie girl?" Mac asked.

"I don't want to go to bed!"

"Why not?"

"Because I don't want to go to bed!"

Lilly cried and squirmed in his arms and he shifted her to a more comfortable position. "What's up with this one?"

"She's overtired and is having a hard time relaxing. Especially with all the noise going on in here."

He nodded. "You take care of Katie. Lilly and I'll be just fine." His words were much braver than he felt, but he was going to do his best.

"Bless you," she said and carried Katie down the hallway to the little girl's room.

Mac turned the baby so he could look into her red face. After snagging a tissue from the end table, he cleaned her up and studied her. "So, kid, it's just you and me."

She stopped crying, and for a brief moment, Mac felt a surge of satisfaction. Then her face crumpled and wails pierced the air once more. "Oh, boy."

He began to pace from one end of the den to the other, talking softly, humming an old Bible school tune he remembered from his childhood, and avoided stepping in front of the windows. All the blinds were pulled, but he wasn't taking any chances.

Five minutes turned into ten that turned into twenty. He finally realized the back of the house was quiet and the baby in his arms had given up her battle with sleep.

He let out a low breath and fatigue hit him hard. He walked over to the recliner and lowered into it, holding Lilly in the crook of his elbow. Her breathing came deep and even, while her muscles twitched every so often.

With a light touch, he traced her a finger over her eyelids, then her nose and puckered lips. Grief gathered in his chest and he closed his eyes. *Lord, I don't know how I'm supposed to heal from this—but I want to.*

It was the first time he'd admitted that to himself. He wanted to live again, to love again, to face the future without dread. To apologize to his sister and make things right with her.

A footstep in the hallway peeled his eyes open. Isabelle stepped into the den and paused when she saw him. Her eyes widened and a tender smile curved her lips. "Oh, my," she said, her voice a whisper. "You did very, very well." He didn't dare laugh. She walked over and took the sleeping baby from his arms. When she did, stray strands of her hair tickled his cheek and he inhaled the scent of her shampoo. A hint of vanilla and something he couldn't identify but definitely liked. Their eyes locked and he swallowed. Isabelle waited a moment, looked like she might say something, then simply smiled once more and straightened.

Lilly stirred at the movement but continued the sleep of the innocent—deep and untroubled. Isabelle disappeared to put the baby in her crib and Mac pulled in a deep breath, ordering his pounding pulse to return to normal.

Why did the woman affect him so?

Before he had a chance to try to come up with an answer, she returned, gave a long sigh and dropped onto the couch. She leaned her head back and closed her eyes. "I'm tired."

"It's just eight o'clock, but you might want to go on to bed while you can." He stood.

"No," she said without opening her eyes. "I have a few more things I need to do before I can sleep."

He paused. "All right. Anything I can do to help?"

"Hmm. No, I don't think so. Unfortunately."

"Okay…then I'll leave you to it."

"I'd rather talk to you."

Her blunt statement left him blinking. "Works for me. What do you want to talk about?"

She patted the sofa cushion next to her and he lowered himself onto it. She rolled her head to look at him. "Tell me about your family. Yourself."

"Why?"

"Because I think you need to."

He huffed a short laugh but bit back the groan. She was probably right. "You're a psychiatrist. Are you going to analyze everything I say?"

"Of course." He paused and she laughed. "No, I'm teasing. I like you, Mac, and I'm curious about you. I can tell you're something of a loner at the moment, at this point in time, but you're a people person—which is probably why you seek out jobs that put you around them."

Okay… "And? What else have you deduced about me?" He wasn't sure whether to be insulted or honored that she'd taken such notice of him.

She studied him and gave a small shrug. "You carry a lot of pain. Your shoulders are strong, but there's a heavy load on them. You mentioned losing your wife and child, so that's probably where that comes from."

"Yeah, it does."

"You like children, but you hold yourself back."

He nodded and looked away. No wonder she was so successful in helping kids. She had a way of looking beneath the surface whether you wanted her to or not. She cleared her throat. "But that's not my business. I'm praying for you, Mac."

That snapped his gaze up to hers. He couldn't

find it in him to protest. He needed her prayers. "Thank you."

She smiled. "Good night, Mac."

She started to go, and he snagged her hand. "Wait."

Isabelle stopped and looked at him with a big question mark in her eyes.

Mac fought to find his voice, to explain his feelings, his thoughts. Isabelle settled back onto the couch but left her hand in his.

"You're right about everything," he said. "I've been running for a long time."

"From your pain?"

He sighed and scraped a hand down his face. "From the truth."

"What truth is that?"

Did he dare say it? He paused. Then, "It's my fault they died."

THIRTEEN

Isabelle froze for a slight second. She'd heard the words, but since they were the last thing she expected him to say, it caught her off guard. He looked away again, and even in the dim light of the room she could make out the flush in his cheeks, the agony in his eyes. "Tell me."

"She shouldn't have been driving that night. We had plans to meet friends for dinner, but we'd had an argument that morning and she'd ignored my calls throughout the day. I thought she was being petty and so when I had a call come in about ten minutes before I was supposed to clock out, I took it. Shortly after that, she called and I let it go to voice mail." Mac rubbed his eyes. "She was trying to get in touch with me to tell me that she was sorry, and she'd canceled the dinner plans and was bringing me dinner so we could eat and talk." He swallowed. "She and Little Mac never made it."

"Oh, Mac, I'm so sorry. So very, very sorry."

"It wasn't even a drunk driver or someone texting and driving. A dog ran out in the road in front of an oncoming car. The driver swerved into my wife's lane and hit her head-on. All three of them died. Jeanie and Little Mac never had a chance and I don't really have anyone to be mad at."

"Except God," she said, "and yourself for not picking up the phone."

"Yeah."

"What would you have said if you'd answered the call?"

He blinked. "What?"

She took his hand. "If you'd picked up the phone and your wife said, 'Mac, I'm sorry we fought. Can I bring you dinner so we can chat?' What would you have said?"

"I would have said…" He let out a shuddering breath and closed his eyes.

"Mac?"

He opened his eyes. "I would have said, 'I'm sorry, too, I'd love for you to bring me dinner.'"

"Which she knew you'd say."

"Which is why she was in the car heading my way," Mac said, his voice low. Tears filled his eyes, but he didn't seem to care. "She was going to be in that car either way, wasn't she?"

"Sounds like it, yes."

"Except if we hadn't fought, I'd have been on my way home."

"Would you really? Or would you have taken the call and let her know you were going to be late?"

He paused. "I... I'm not sure."

"I think you are."

For a moment, he stared at his hands, thinking. "Maybe. I'd done it before, of course. When someone needs help, you don't ignore it, no matter how close to going home you are."

She squeezed his fingers. "Because that's the kind of man you are."

He eyed her. "You're too easy to talk to."

A laugh slipped from her. Short and low. "Do I say thanks or apologize?"

When a small smile curved his lips, joy lit up inside her. He might blame himself, but he was working toward seeing that it wasn't true.

"Before I started my shift, I called her and left a voice mail that I regretted the fight. I even sent her a few texts. She never answered and it made me mad."

"And hurt."

"Yes." He drew in a deep breath. "But turns out she'd lost her phone and had only found it shortly before she called me. I felt like dirt, but we both knew things would be all right, eventually. Only—" he shook his head "—we never got to eventually."

"Can you see it wasn't your fault, though? It was an accident. A stupid, tragic accident."

He nodded. "Mentally, I know, I just…" He raked a hand over his head. "Tell me about your husband."

She blinked at the sudden change of subject. Isabelle had tons to do for the Day at the Ranch event, but she decided this was more important for the moment. "I've told you most everything. There's not much more to tell. Josiah was a wonderful man and we were mostly happy even though we had our ups and downs like all couples. The one thing that would have been the icing on the cake, so to speak, would have been to have children. When it didn't happen, we fostered. And then he died, and I'm keeping the dream going."

"How are you doing that? It seems terribly overwhelming."

She let out a low laugh. "Oh, it's overwhelming all right." She pressed her thumb and forefinger to her eyes and thought about what to say. When she looked up, he was simply sitting patiently, watching her. "You're pretty easy to talk to yourself, you know?"

"That's a good thing, then."

Was it? Isabelle wasn't stupid. She knew what

was going on with her emotions. She was falling for this man. The problem was, he wasn't planning on sticking around and she was heading straight for heartbreak. To let herself believe anything else was foolish. She gave a slight shrug. "I have an offer from someone to buy the land."

"You're thinking of selling?"

"Well…not every day. But yes, occasionally, I think about it. I could go back into practice treating patients and still be a foster mother without this property to worry about."

He frowned. "But you love this place."

"I really do."

"But?"

"But it's a lot of work, a lot of stress, a lot of…everything. However, I feel like if I sell or even give the property back to my parents, I'd be giving up." She bit her lip. "I don't know what to do some days."

"Is keeping the place going a way of keeping Josiah with you? The feeling that you'd be letting him down if you gave it up?"

"Studied some psychology yourself, have you?"

"It came in handy with the police job."

"I'm sure." She sighed. "Trust me, I've thought about that, but no. Josiah wouldn't want me to feel that way. He'd want me to do whatever was best for me at this point in time. He'd never push his dream on me."

He looked like she'd slapped him.

"Mac?" She held his hand while he processed whatever was going through his head. "What is it?"

He blinked and shook his head. "Nothing. I just…was thinking."

"About?"

"The fact that Jeanie would want the same for me." He shook his head. He stood. "I'd better let you get some work done or rest."

She nodded and rose to stand next to him. "You're healing here, Mac. I hope you'll stay for a while if only for that."

He drew in a deep breath and brought a hand up to cup her cheek. "You're a very special person, Isabelle Trent. I'm honored to have met you." She kept her gaze on his. His eyes dropped to her lips and she stilled. Waiting. Then he cleared his throat and took a step back.

Isabelle did the same. "Can I ask you a question before you go?"

"Of course."

"Do you think you'll ever settle down again? Let your heart be open to love again?"

Mac hesitated, then shook his head. "I don't know. If you'd asked me that question a month ago, the answer would have been a flat no, but I think I'm getting tired."

"Tired of running from the pain?"

He smiled. A sad, lopsided curving of his lips. "That's one way of looking at it, I suppose. What about you?"

"Love again? Yes. I'm not looking for it to happen, but if it's meant to be and God sends that person my way, then I'll love again with my whole heart."

Pain flashed. "I admire that."

"What would your wife tell you?"

He let out a low laugh. "That I'm being an idiot and to do whatever makes me happy—including living my life and finding love again."

"You didn't even hesitate when you said that."

"No," he said, his voice soft, thoughtful. "I guess I didn't."

"She and Josiah sound like they would have gotten along very well." She paused. "I don't know if you want my advice, but here it is. You can't outrun the pain. I know this from experience. It won't seem like it at first, but it's much better to face it head-on and deal with it. Only then will you be able to see past it."

He dropped his gaze and shoved his hands in his pockets. Isabelle bit her lip, thinking she'd said too much. Then he sighed. "Good night, Isabelle, I'll see you in the morning."

He turned to walk away, and Isabelle reached out to stop him, then dropped her hand. She'd been the one to open up the conversation, but he'd closed it. She'd respect that.

She took another look out the window and sent up one more prayer that tonight would be a quiet one. However, as tired as she was, sleep would elude her, so she might as well work. She went to the kitchen and started a fresh pot of coffee, then she went to the door and stuck her head out. "Grant, you okay? You can come in, you know. I'm making coffee."

"Thanks, but I want to be seen if this guy decides to come visiting. I could use some coffee, though."

Just as she was about to offer to get it for him, Mac joined them on the porch. "Thought you were going to bed," she said.

"If I could sleep, I would. Since I'm awake, I figured I might as well be useful." He nodded to Grant. "You need to take a break?"

Grant stood. "Sure. Just for a few minutes. Thanks." He smiled at Isabelle. "I'll get the coffee. You go on to bed and get some rest."

Rest? She looked out over the property that had always been a source of peace and comfort for her. Tonight, a shiver rippled through her and a sense of danger wiped out any thoughts of rest.

* * *

Mac woke to the smell of bacon, eggs and cinnamon. But most important, coffee. His stomach immediately rumbled and he rolled out of bed to shower and dress. Ten minutes later, cup in hand, he walked out onto the porch to find Grant leaning against the nearest post, sipping out of a travel mug, and Isabelle sitting in one of the rockers with baby Lilly in her arms. The child waved a chew toy and babbled at Mac when he sat in the chair next to them. He propped his boots on the rail and tapped Lilly on the nose. "Morning," he said. "Glad to see she's in a better mood."

Isabelle shot him a quick smile. "Good morning. Sleep can do wonders for one's disposition. Not to mention a lovely day." She glanced at the sky. "It's going to be a pretty one. Not a raindrop in sight."

She sounded chipper enough, but the dark shadows under her eyes told the real story. "Didn't sleep much, huh?"

"I look that bad?"

He blinked. "What? No, not at all."

"Liar." Her gentle rebuke pulled a chuckle from him. Why was it he found himself smiling every time he was around her? In spite of the chaos they were involved in? He wasn't sure of the answer, but he decided it might be inter-

esting to find out. The thought sent shards of…
something through him. Fear? Terror? Hope?
Longing?

"Mac?" Isabelle asked.

He shook himself. "Yeah?"

"You okay?"

"Of course." He looked at Grant. "Hope you
got some rest last night."

Grant covered a smile and shot him a knowing look. "Thanks to you and your three-hour
shift."

"Happy to do it." Mac worked on emptying
the coffee cup, ignoring the heat climbing into
his cheeks. He'd have to learn how to hide his
feelings a little better. And he'd thought he was
pretty good at it.

"I called Social Services this morning," Isabelle said.

All embarrassment fled and Mac lowered his
feet with a thump to lean toward her. "You did
what?"

Grant made a low noise of surprise but didn't
comment.

Isabelle looked away, then back at them. "It
was one of the hardest things I've ever done,"
she said, "but, after that bull incident—" She
broke off and swallowed. "Katie could have
been killed. Last night, I was thinking about
it and praying about it and I feel like it's the

only option." Tears filled her pretty eyes and she blinked them away. "It's the only smart— and loving—thing to do. I also told the kids everything about Lilly and why someone's been causing trouble. I also explained that they would be coming back just as soon as it was safe for them to be here. The bus is on the way to pick them up for school. After school, Cheryl will take them to a safe house."

"What about Lilly?" Mac asked.

"She'll be staying here with me," Isabelle said. "Her father—" She stopped and grimaced. "I don't want to call him that. He doesn't deserve that title. Drew is only after her, but it's obvious he doesn't mind hurting people who might stand in his way to *get* her. As long as the other children aren't with her, I feel like they'll be safe."

"And we'll guard Lilly here," Grant said with a nod. "It's a good plan."

"Yeah," Mac said, his voice low. "That makes sense. I hate that it's necessary, but I think you're wise to do that."

"It's definitely not what I want," Isabelle said, "but they come first. Their safety is the priority."

"What did the kids say?"

She shot him a thoughtful smile. "You know, I thought about trying to convince them that they were going on a little vacation for a few days, but they're way smarter than that." She shook her head. "And they've been lied to so much of their short lives that I couldn't do it. I thought honesty was the best policy in this case—even with Katie. They're worried, of course, but not about me not wanting them here. They understand that I don't want to send them away, that I'm doing it out of love, and they'll be back soon. They have complete confidence in Grant and Ben." She looked at Mac. "And you."

The trust in her eyes and the care on her face nearly sent Mac's heart over the edge. What had happened to his walls? How had he allowed his defenses to be breached?

Because he'd wanted to? Subconsciously, maybe? Isabelle was right. He *was* healing here. He cleared his throat and glanced at Grant. "What's being done to find this guy?"

"We're working with local authorities and the university where he and Zoe were students. They're keeping an eye out for him to show up. We're also tracking his phone but haven't got a hit on it. If he's using a cellular device, it's one we don't know about."

"Could be a burner," Mac said.

"Exactly. We're also monitoring Zoe's phone. He's left her some pretty harsh and threatening messages." Grant's eye darkened and he looked at the infant giggling in Isabelle's lap. "There's no way we can let this guy get his hands on that baby. He said in one of his texts that he was going to take Lilly and make sure that Zoe never saw her again. His one goal is to get revenge on the girl that dumped him—and if that means hurting an innocent baby, then he doesn't care."

Isabelle shuddered and Mac's muscles clenched. Grant was right. They had to stop Drew before he finally succeeded in his lethal quest.

FOURTEEN

For Isabelle, the hours passed slowly. She found herself checking the time every fifteen to thirty minutes even while she entertained the baby, did four loads of laundry and cleaned the three and a half bathrooms while Lilly napped. Now the baby was wide-awake, spending her time darting about the house in her walker.

However, no matter what might distract her for a few moments, Isabelle's mind kept coming back to the issue at hand. She wished she could do something, anything, to help find Drew Baldwin and get the children returned, but what could she do?

She'd also love to visit Zoe, but again, that wasn't an option. As the sun dropped without the children's shouts, laughter and the occasional fight, sadness gripped her.

Her phone buzzed and she snagged it from her pocket. "Hello?"

"Isabelle. Hi." Regina's voice came on.

"What's going on? How are you? How are things at the ranch? Talk to me."

"Bored much?" Isabelle asked.

"You don't even know. Seriously, how are things at your place?"

"Quiet. For now."

Isabelle stood at the kitchen window, watching the tree line in the distance, straining to see any sign of light or life that would indicate Drew was going to try again. The fact that the dogs ran in the pasture and showed no signs of agitation soothed her worry somewhat.

"Quiet is good," Regina said. "I thought I'd come over and kind of be another set of eyes if that's okay with you."

"Are you sure you feel like it?"

"I can be in pain at home or be in pain at your place. At least you'll be a distraction."

"Then, by all means, come on over."

"Great. See you soon."

Isabelle hung up and tossed one more glance outside. *Please, God, keep him away. Or, if he gets close, let him get caught. This has to end. Those children don't deserve this.* The prayer whispered upward.

Isabelle checked on Lilly, who'd figured out a new game with the walker. She churned her little legs until the walker ran into the wall and bounced her backward. Her chuckles peeled through the room, making Isabelle smile. The fact that her lips curved up in spite of everything brought her a slight measure of peace. "You're a funny kid, Lilly," Isabelle said.

A knock sounded just before the door opened and she turned to see Mac step inside. He pulled off his gloves and stood on the mat in stocking feet. He must have taken his boots off outside so as to not track in dirt. That kind of consideration drew her to him even more. "I finally finished fixing that fence," he said.

"Wonderful. Thank you."

"Ben's back. Grant went on home. Cody Ray and Ms. Sybil are heading to the café in town." He paused. "Are they...together? Like a couple?"

She laughed. "Yes. They've been friends for a long time, so the romance thing is kind of new for them. They're just enjoying each other's company and taking it slow."

"That's really nice." A funny look flashed across his face.

"What is it?"

"I guess I find it kind of amusing they're taking it slow. I mean, at their age, you would think you'd know if it was right or not, wouldn't you?"

Isabelle fought a grin. "I'm not sure how it works at that age. I'm not sure how it works at *our* age. Josiah and I were high school sweethearts. We went to the same college, graduated on the same day, got jobs in the same town." She shrugged. "Marriage just seemed to be the next step." She paused. "Sounds really boring, doesn't it?"

"Absolutely not. It sounds…nice."

Nice, but not terribly exciting. "What about you? How did you and your wife meet?"

"At the church singles group." This time it was his turn to pause. "I guess that sounds boring, too."

"Well, when you think about how you and I met, I'll take boring any day of the week." It hit her what that sounded like and heat engulfed her cheeks. "Um, not that you and I are… I mean… I didn't mean to make it sound like—" She drew in a breath. "I think I'm going to shut up now."

A small smile tugged at his lips. "We did have a pretty exciting first meeting, didn't we?"

"We did." *Please, change the subject so I don't have to crawl in a hole and hide.*

Lilly chose that moment to aim her walker at Mac's shins. He jumped out of the way at the last minute and grabbed the toy turned projectile. "Whoa, there, little girl." Lilly chuckled and Mac turned her in the other direction. She took off like a missile.

"Ben and I talked," Mac said, "and he suggested I hang out inside with you and Lilly while he keeps an eye on everything outside."

"That sounds good. Come on in and have a seat. Or better yet, redirect Lilly before she puts a dent in the wall."

Mac laughed. "But she's having so much fun."

Lilly squealed and rammed the wall again. She bounced back and grinned at them like she expected to be praised.

Mac walked over to her and lifted her out of the walker. "Come on, kid, before you give yourself whiplash."

Lilly grabbed his nose and pulled.

Isabelle's heart tumbled all over the place. She could watch the two of them forever. A lump gathered in her throat. But she wouldn't have either of them for that long. *Don't think about that. Be grateful for the time you have.* She cleared her throat. "Regina's on her way over. Said she wanted to be another set of eyes."

"She feels well enough to do that?"

"Probably not."

"Ah. She's one of those type A people?"

"Hmm."

"Sounds like someone else I know."

Isabelle chuckled. "I guess it comes with being an only child."

"And Regina? Is she an only child?"

"Oh, no. She wishes she was, sometimes. She has four older brothers, and the sheriff is her cousin."

"Oh, wow. Poor woman."

"No kidding."

Lilly gave a half cry and stuffed her fingers into her mouth. "I think someone's getting hungry," Mac said.

"I've got her food ready to warm up."

"Want me to put her in the highchair?"

Isabelle raised a brow. "Sure."

While Mac got the child settled in her chair, Isabelle warmed the food and watched the two of them from the corner of her eye. He played peekaboo with Lilly, distracting her momentarily from her hunger. For a moment, Isabelle let herself envision the three of them as a family, then sucked in a deep breath and shoved the image away. *They're not yours. They're leaving.*

Unfortunately, they were going to take her heart with them when they did.

Mac spooned another scoop of something that looked like a cross between mashed potatoes and green beans into the baby's mouth. She swallowed, kicked her feet and opened her mouth for more. He obliged. She thanked him by blowing a raspberry—and everything that he'd just put in her mouth. The combination hit him in the cheek, the eye, the forehead—and his hair.

He jumped back with a startled "Hey!"

Lilly froze, eyes wide, then erupted into giggles.

Isabelle spun, met his gaze and swallowed. She bit her lip and Mac could tell she was desperately trying not to laugh. "Could I get a towel?"

"Absolutely."

"You can laugh."

"I wouldn't think of it." The words came out slightly choked.

When the knock sounded on the door, signaling Regina's arrival, Isabelle tossed him the towel and darted to the door.

Once Regina had taken over Lilly's feeding, Mac went to his room to get the last remaining bits of baby food out of his hair.

In the bathroom, he pulled the washcloth over his head, then set it on the counter and closed his eyes. His chin dropped to his chest and he stood there. Thinking. Feeling. There was no more denying that his heart was invested in the people on this ranch. He wasn't quite sure exactly how it had happened. But it had. Which meant he had decisions to make. In the time that he'd been at the ranch, he'd made a lot of improvements on the property. He'd replaced the fence, fixed the sabotaged one, helped Cody Ray repair the flooring in the barn, upgraded the security system, changed the oil in all of the ranch vehicles, moved the small herd of cows to a different grazing area—and more. Cody Ray took care of the horses and other animals, of course, so if he left, and it took Isabelle a few weeks to hire someone else, she should be all right.

With his next paycheck, he'd have enough for a down payment on that land he'd had his eye on. Then he'd build his home.

He looked up and stared himself in the eye.

Build it for what? For whom?

For the first time since he'd set out on his journey—okay, since he'd decided to run from life and the pain of his loss—he allowed himself to picture what that would look like.

Building the house would keep him distracted for the most part, but what about when it was finished? What then?

He envisioned himself sitting in his recliner, watching sports on the big-screen television he'd have over the fireplace. Meals would be eaten at the table big enough for eight. But who would fill the other chairs? The bleak picture sent shards of pain and regret through him.

He spun from the mirror—and his thoughts—to step into the small living area. He wanted to pace, but the room limited him to standing in front of the fireplace.

He walked to the window and looked over the land. The sun had set some time ago, but he could see the lights from the barn casting a soft glow around it. While he was watching, a shadow stepped around the corner and he tensed until he realized it was Ben. Glad the man was being diligent about patrolling and keeping an eye on things, Mac returned to his brooding.

What was he going to do?

He sighed. The first thing he was going to do was stop thinking. He returned to the living area to find Regina seated on the couch, talking on her phone, and Isabelle cleaning up the baby. She glanced up at him. "Lilly's willing to try again if you're game."

He held up a hand. "We both know how that'll end. Thankfully, it looks like she's all finished." He paused. "But if she needs rocking to sleep, I'm your volunteer."

Isabelle stopped and studied him. "Be careful, Mac," she said, her voice soft. "You might find it hard to leave when the time comes."

He narrowed his eyes. "I'm just offering to rock her."

"Uh-huh."

Mac ignored the heat he could feel climbing into his neck. "Well?"

Isabelle lifted the baby out of the high chair and passed her to Mac. "She might want to play a bit first."

"We can do that while you and Regina visit." Regina had hung up and was eyeing Mac with a knowing look. What was it with the deputies and their keen instincts? He hid a grimace. It was the cop in them, no doubt.

He narrowed his eyes at Regina, who ducked her head to hide a smile. Mac ignored her and took Lilly into the den, where he settled her on the floor with toys and soft books. He read three of them to her when she wasn't grabbing them and throwing them across the room for him to chase down.

In the background, he could hear Regina and Isabelle discussing the upcoming weekend and the Day at the Ranch. Their voices faded as he played with Lilly until she started rubbing her eyes. He picked her up and carried her into her little room and lowered them into the rocking chair. While he rocked, she babbled and tried to stay awake, but finally, she succumbed to sleep.

And Mac fought the emotions that once again threatened to engulf him. He needed to call his sister and apologize.

Then he'd make arrangements to go see her and meet his new niece in person at the earliest possible opportunity. He wasn't sure exactly when that would be, but he knew it wouldn't be before he was absolutely certain Isabelle and the kids were safe.

FIFTEEN

Lilly was sleeping thanks to Mac, the baby whisperer. The other children were safe, Regina was keeping watch while Ben snagged a few hours of sleep in the bunkhouse near the barn, and Isabelle needed to get some rest herself. But after two hours of tossing and turning, she finally gave up.

She pulled on sweatpants and a long-sleeved T-shirt over her sleep clothes, wondering if she should try warm milk for the first time in her life. She hated the idea, but she was getting desperate enough to see if there was any merit to the old wives' tale.

Or she could clean the kitchen. She slid her phone into the front pocket of her sweats and slipped out of her bedroom on quiet feet. Then remembered she only had one child in the house. Heaviness settled over her. *Please, God, let this trouble come to an end. I want those kids back home. They need to be here.*

Keeping the lights off, Isabelle walked into the room and over to the window that gave her a view of the wooded area beyond the yard. She stood on the side to peer out. No sense in giving Drew Baldwin a clear shot should he be watching.

"Hey."

The soft voice made her jump. She spun to see Regina sitting on the couch. "I thought you were keeping watch."

"I was, but Ben said he couldn't sleep, so I made myself comfortable."

"There's a lot of that unable-to-sleep thing going on tonight," Isabelle murmured. From her position near the window she could see that the lights from the barn burned brighter than usual. Too bright. She frowned.

A hazy fog, visible thanks to the barn lights, had settled over the roof and Isabelle watched it for a moment, wondering at the odd sight. Realization hit her along with the panic. "Oh, no. Oh, no. No, no, no!"

Regina shot to her feet. "What is it?"

"I think the barn's on fire!" Isabelle raced to the porch. "Ben! Cody Ray!"

"Isabelle! I see it!" Ben's cry came from the side of the barn. "The pasture's on fire and the flames are heading toward the barn! Call 911! I'm getting the hose!"

The dogs raced from the bunkhouse. Cody Ray followed, with a fire extinguisher in one hand and another strapped to his back. That might buy them some time, but only for a bit. "Milo, Sugar, house!" The dogs stopped, turned and hurried back to the house as ordered. Only Sugar looked back over her shoulder and sat. Cody Ray seemed satisfied they would stay out of harm's way and dashed to the flames licking up the field, eating their way toward the barn.

Isabelle dug her phone from her pocket, dialed 911 and reported the fire. She turned back to Regina, who stood in the doorway, jaw tight, eyes narrowed. "I don't know what's happening," Isabelle said, "but please watch over Lilly."

"Don't you need my help with the fire?"

"You've got one arm right now. I need you here more, protecting Lilly."

"Fine, fine. I've got her." She hesitated for a fraction. "I'm going to get her and keep her with me in the cruiser just in case this is some kind of distraction to get everyone away from the house."

"Good idea. Can you manage her with one arm?"

"I can. I can actually use the injured one with some pain, but I'll be fine. Get Mac and go!"

Still, Isabelle hesitated. "You're positive?"

"I'll keep her safe, Isabelle, I promise. Do

what you have to do to help the men with the fire."

"Thank you." Isabelle raced around to Mac's door and pounded. "Mac!"

The door flew open. "I heard." He was pulling on his gloves. "I should stay here. This could be a distraction to get most everyone away from the house to get to Lilly."

Great minds and all that. "We've already got that covered." She aimed for the barn, explaining briefly that Regina was taking care of the baby. She hurried to find Cody Ray holding one hose and spraying the barn while Ben worked with the other to douse the flames creeping toward the fence. "I've got to let the horses out!"

"Right behind you," Mac said.

Isabelle darted into the barn to find the horses restless, pacing and pawing at their stall doors. Smoke filled the area, leaking in through the open windows. Starting at the end nearest the pasture that was away from the fire, she opened the door. "Come on, big guy. Go!" She slapped his hindquarters as he bolted out. The smoke continued to pour in. She coughed and bent at the waist, trying to get lower. She found a pocket of fresh air and dragged it in, then moved to Maverick's stall. One by one, she got the horses out on her side of the stable while Mac worked the other side.

In the distance she could finally hear the sirens and prayed they arrived before the flames reached the barn.

"Isabelle? You okay?" Mac's voice came from the other end of the building.

"I'm okay. One more horse, and then we can get out of here."

"I've got him," he said. Through the thickening smoke, she saw him heading for the last stall. She tried to draw in a breath and got a lungful of smoke that sent her into a coughing fit.

"Get out, Isabelle!"

She had no choice. She couldn't breathe. But she couldn't leave Mac. "Just hurry," she pleaded. She dropped to the dirt floor and found the air still smoky, but better. She managed to grab a lungful, then shot to her feet. "Mac?"

"Go!"

"Where are you?" She let out another cough, feeling like she was suffocating. Flames flickered from the other end of the barn and terror seized her. "Mac! We have to go now!"

"I'm right behind you." He sounded a little farther away than that, but good enough. Isabelle headed for the door, following the last horse. Right before the exit, the mare whinnied and reared, coming down hard. Isabelle scurried backward and then around to the side. She started to grab the halter when the horse reared again, knocking her back. She slammed into the stall wall and sat there for a brief second to regain her senses. Choking and wheezing, she stumbled to her feet and slapped the horse on the flank.

Her lungs burned, and her eyes streamed tears from the smoke.

She burst outside and was hit in the face with a blast of water from the hose. Sputtering, she nevertheless let it wet her lips and tongue while she stole a quick look to make sure Mac was truly right behind her. She didn't see him, but she couldn't see much of anything at the moment. "Mac!" The word came out a croak rather than the yell she'd intended.

Cody Ray hurried over to her. "Rinse your eyes and your face, hon."

She did so, only to clear her vision. She needed to see. "Mac didn't come out."

Two fire trucks raced up the drive. Even before the wheels stopped turning, firefighters were unloading from the vehicle. Their shouted orders carried through the smoky haze and they scrambled into action.

Cody Ray fell back, as did Ben.

Isabelle surveyed the flames licking at the side of the barn. Where was Mac? As if she'd summoned him, he appeared in the opening of the building and staggered out, holding Milo. Cody Ray let out a short yell and met Mac as he raced toward them. Cody took the dog. "I didn't know he'd gotten away."

"He's okay," Mac rasped, then let out a long cough. The dog proved his words by letting out a bark even though he was panting hard.

One of the paramedics hurried over with an oxygen mask and slapped it on Mac's face. Then did the same for Isabelle. She pulled in a deep breath and let her gaze roam the faces around her. Then the property. Someone had started that fire. She didn't have any proof other than the feeling in her gut. She had to check on Lilly and Regina.

With everyone preoccupied with putting the fire out, Isabelle pulled off the oxygen mask and made her way through the chaos to Regina's cruiser.

As she passed the nearest fire truck, she caught movement from the corner of her eye. She spun toward it and something slammed into her shoulder, sending her crashing to the ground with a cry.

Mac had gotten a good dose of the smoke, but after inhaling the oxygen and clearing his lungs, he started to feel better. His main concern was Isabelle. In all of the chaos, he didn't want to lose sight of her. Only he had. He ripped the mask from his face. "Isabelle?" A faint cry reached him and he whirled to see Isabelle go down. He bolted toward her. "Isabelle!"

A dark figure peeled away from the fire truck and darted for the tree line. "Not this time, buddy," he muttered. "Isabelle, are you okay?"

"Yes, get him!" She stumbled to her feet and Mac altered his course slightly, keeping the black-hooded man in his sights. The guy was fast, but determination burned in Mac's blood. He pushed hard, running full out, dodging anything that might trip him up.

The guy scrambled over the fence.

"Police! Stop!"

Ben's cry came from behind him. Glad he had backup, Mac kept going, his boots pounding the ground, closing the distance. He came to the fence and never slowed. At the right moment, he placed his hands on the top board and vaulted over in a copycat move.

At the tree line, the figure stumbled, tried to right himself, then went down. He started to roll to his feet, but Mac was faster. He dove a shoulder into the man on the ground. The impact jarred him, the pain of the contact shooting through his arm and into his neck. But he heard the breath whoosh from the man's lungs as he jerked, choking, and gasping to breathe. Mac rolled to his knees, reached out and ripped the hoodie away from the guy's head. "Drew Baldwin," Mac said between gritted teeth. "Nice to meet you."

Ben reached them and Mac shoved his prisoner back to the ground and yanked his hands behind his back. Ben cuffed him, and Mac sat back to catch his breath. He was more winded than that little run should have made him, and he figured he had the smoke to thank for that.

Coughing, he stood and helped Ben get Baldwin on his feet. "You're done."

Baldwin snarled. "Lilly's mine. No one's keeping me away from her."

"Right. You keep telling yourself that while you're sitting behind bars."

The guy lunged at him, but Ben yanked him back. "Stop it. You're not going anywhere. Make things easier on yourself. You're already looking at attempted murder. Want to add resisting arrest to the charges?"

His words brought Baldwin to a stop. "What are you talking about?"

Ben pushed him forward. "Not to mention attempted kidnapping."

"She's my kid! It's not kidnapping if she belongs to me. You can't keep me from my own child. I have rights!"

"Yes, you do," Ben said. "Why don't I tell

them to you right now?" He did while Baldwin protested throughout the recitation.

Mac ignored the sputtering man. And when Ben was done and Baldwin had agreed he understood his rights, Mac pointed to the barn. "That your handiwork?"

A shrug from Baldwin sent Mac's fingers curling into a fist. He forcibly relaxed them and took a deep breath. Then coughed. It would take a while for the effects of the smoke to wear off. "Oh, yeah, you've got a lot of charges coming your way."

"Mac!" Isabelle ran toward them, her eye wide. "You got him."

"We did. Ben and I made a good team." He shot her a slight smile, but her eyes never wavered from the man in custody.

"Finally," she breathed. "It's over."

"I'll get out," Baldwin said. "I'll be back."

She raised a brow. "I guess we'll see about that. I'm sure attempted murder will be taken a bit more seriously than the trespassing charge, but you won't be back anytime soon."

"Why does everyone keep talking about attempted murder? I haven't tried to kill anyone. I just wanted my baby."

"Yeah, so you can really stick it to Zoe, right?"

Isabelle looked ready to deck the guy herself,

so Mac stepped in and took her hand in his. "Don't argue with him, Isabelle. He's going to deny all but probably the lesser charges."

"Like kidnapping and arson?"

"Something like that."

"I didn't try to murder anyone!" They had reached Ben's cruiser. Ben opened the door and pushed the man into the back seat. "I'm telling you I didn't try to kill anyone!" Baldwin shouted.

"Because running me and a friend down in the middle of a crosswalk was going to be good for our health?"

"What are you talking about?"

"Throwing a hammer through the window of my van was helpful?"

"Hey, I was just trying to distract you, that's all. I wasn't trying to hit you."

"Kicking the fence down so the bull could get out and come terrorize—and possibly kill—a five-year-old? How about that one? That's attempted murder in my book."

"I didn't kick any fence down. What bull?"

"Come on," Ben said. "We'll work all this out at the station. You have a lawyer?"

"No. I don't need one."

"Yes, you do."

"You just read me my rights. I don't have to

have a lawyer. I don't need one because I haven't done anything wrong."

Was the kid really that stupid?

Ben slammed the door and Baldwin's words were cut off. Ben opened the driver's door and slid into the seat. "If you want to come down to the station and listen to the interrogation, Creed will probably let you. I mean, you did tackle the guy."

"You can take the man out of the uniform," Mac said, "but once a cop always a cop, I guess."

"If you're sticking around and want to get back to it full-time, talk to Creed. He's got the money to hire two more deputies."

Mac's heart leaped and he squelched it as reality hit him. Isabelle and the children were safe now, his work on the ranch was pretty much done, and he had enough money to put the down payment on his land. He could leave anytime now.

Why wasn't he a lot more happy about that? "Thanks, but I've got plans of my own and they don't include law enforcement." And yet, he couldn't help the surge of adrenaline at the thought. Bringing down Drew Baldwin had been incredibly satisfying. "Shoot me a text if Creed says it's all right for me to be there when he questions the guy." He would be observing behind the interrogation room mirror, but that was all right. And then he could leave when he felt like it was time, without worrying that Isabelle and the children were in danger. For some reason, the thought didn't bring the relief he thought it would.

Ben nodded and shut the door. Mac turned to Isabelle and caught her frown. "What is it?"

"Why do I have the feeling that you're thinking of leaving?"

He wouldn't lie to her. "I've thought about it, but I've still got a few things to do around here. We have a Day at the Ranch to put on."

Her eyes smiled at him. "Yes, we do." She paused. "And, Mac? If you feel it's time to leave, you don't have to give me thirty days."

Her words shot arrows through his heart, but there was something more than the thought of leaving. Something else wasn't sitting right with him, but he couldn't put his finger on it. He just knew it had to do with Drew Baldwin and the man's many protestations about some of the incidents that had involved Isabelle. Why would he freely admit to attempting to kidnap his own kid, yet deny he tried to kill Isabelle?

Because he thought a jury would have more mercy on a father who just wanted to be with his child? Mac had no doubt Drew Baldwin couldn't care less about raising his daughter and that he was only going after her to spite Zoe, but for a jury, he'd play the loving father who'd been done wrong by his vicious girlfriend.

He might not be as stupid as Mac thought. Maybe he was actually being incredibly smart and was already setting up how his defense would play out. That had to be it.

What else could it be?

SIXTEEN

Something was wrong, and for the life of her, Isabelle couldn't pin down where her anxiety was coming from. She should be relaxed and happy. She'd had the best night's sleep since… well, it seemed like forever, and she'd just talked to Cheryl, who was bringing the children home after school. They'd be here for the Day at the Ranch festival tomorrow, which should have had her jumping for joy. And she *was* happy. *Very* happy.

And yet…

Isabelle took a sip of her coffee and looked out over her land, trying to convince her troubled soul that all was well. "Lord, give me peace," she whispered. "Or tell me why I'm still antsy." While the restless feeling never dissipated, she felt better for the prayer. And for one thing that she'd finally settled on early this morning, after talking to the children on the phone and hearing their excitement about coming back.

There was no way she was going to sell. Not now, not ever.

This was home. She was doing what she was supposed to be doing, and just because it was hard and overwhelming at times, it didn't mean she should give up and quit. She'd admitted one more thing, as well. She wanted to adopt the kids. All of them. It was a complete long shot, but not out of the realm of possibility. Katie's father was going to be in prison for life for murder and her mother was a drug addict who couldn't get straight. Danny's parents had been killed in an auto accident and simply had no other family to care for him. Zeb's background was closer to Katie's. So there was the real likelihood that she could wind up with one—or all—of the children on a permanent basis. But for now, she waited.

Mac's door opened and her heart did that funny little beat when he was around. She'd fallen for the man but was trying to tell herself it was just because he'd saved her life a few times.

She grimaced. Ah, who was she kidding? She was going to be heartbroken when he left. And her heart said that was going to be sooner rather than later.

She forced a smile when he sat next to her and propped his boots on the railing. "How are you this morning?" he asked.

"Sore. Trying not to think about my still smoldering part of the barn and pasture. But I'm all right. What about you?"

"Other than the occasional cough, I'm fine. And glad this is all over."

"Me, too." She couldn't hold the smile and it slipped back into a frown.

"What is it?" he asked.

"I'm not sure, to be honest. I still have a very unsettled feeling in the pit of my stomach."

He sipped his coffee. "It's been a rough time, Isabelle. It's not any wonder that you might still be having some anxiety about everything that happened."

Was that it? Just some sort of weird PTSD thing? She forced the smile back on her face. "You're probably right."

He studied her. "But you don't think so."

She shrugged, a small lift of her shoulders. "I don't know, Mac. I keep going back to Drew Baldwin's admission about some of the things and his denial about others."

"I'm going to sit in on the questioning in about an hour. Why don't you come with me?"

"You think they'll let me?"

"I don't see why not. If anyone has a right to listen to what that man has to say, I'd think it would be you."

She nodded. "I'll text Creed."

"Good."

She sent the text, then said, "The kids are coming back after school. I talked to them this morning and Katie asked if you were still here."

"I'm still here."

She faced him. "And I'm glad for that."

Mac lifted a hand to her cheek and his eyes held hers for a long moment. She could clearly see that he wanted to kiss her but was giving her time to back away if she didn't want him to. In the span of those few seconds, Isabelle considered the fact that he was leaving even though he knew she wanted him to stay.

Maybe she needed to make that exceptionally clear.

She leaned forward and he met her in the middle to close his lips over hers. She stilled for a split second at the touch, then returned the kiss, hoping she revealed the contents of her heart in the gentle exploration.

When he lifted his head, the storm clouds in his eyes saddened her—and gladdened her in a weird way. He was conflicted. Part of him wanted to stay, while the other part was urging him to go before he got his heart broken once again. Maybe he just needed some time. "Why did you want to kiss me when you're already planning on leaving?" she asked.

He cleared his throat. "I'm not sure. I haven't

kissed anyone since my wife died and, honestly, I wasn't sure I could."

"So that was an experiment?"

"What? No. No way. Please don't think that. I'm…floundering. I'm sorry." He stood. "Isabelle, I think you're a beautiful, amazing woman, and I've never met anyone quite like you."

"Not even your wife?"

He smiled. "You have some of the same qualities, of course. You're kind, you think about others before yourself, you always try to do the right thing. Those kinds of things. But you're also very different. Jeanie could never have run a place like this. Organization was definitely not her strong point." He shrugged and drained his cup. "You're two different people and I'm starting to see that's okay."

"Oh." She cleared her throat. "Well…um… that's good." It was, right? "I don't want you to leave, Mac," she finally said, her voice soft.

He closed his eyes for a split second as though her words had pained him. "I know. I'm not sure I want to, either, but trying to figure out if I *have* to."

Before she could ask him to clarify that confusing statement, he rose. "I'm going to check and make sure everything in the barn is ready for tomorrow. The dunking booth is arriving in an hour, and Cody Ray said he'd get it where it belongs."

Tears surged to the surface and she blinked them back. "Thank you. You've done an incredible job around here. I can't tell you how much I appreciate it."

He nodded. "You're welcome. I'm going to go grab my key, then we can head to town if that works for you."

"Sounds good to me. Want me to take your cup?"

He handed it to her and when she took it, his fingers grazed hers, then lingered like his gaze. "Thank you."

She swallowed. "Of course."

Mac left and Isabelle drew in a slow breath while her heart thudded faster than usual. "Stop it," she muttered. "He just said he was leaving." And she'd better start working on a way to protect her heart so it didn't shatter when he drove away.

Once inside the kitchen, she found Lilly in her high chair and Ms. Sybil pulling fresh rolls from the oven. "You spoil us, my dear friend."

The woman laughed. "Well, they weren't really for y'all. They're for the festival tomorrow. Then I decided that would be kind of mean, so made an extra batch."

Isabelle kissed the woman's cheek and snatched

a hot roll. She juggled it on her way to her room, where she grabbed her purse. By the time she returned to the den to find Mac waiting, she could finally manage a bite of the tasty bread. "Oh, that's so good. Did you get one?"

"One?" Ms. Sybil asked. "He's already downed four."

Isabelle laughed. "I hope your extra batch was extra big." She tickled Lilly under her chin and the baby grinned at her. With her heart in her throat, she nodded to Mac that she was ready, and headed for the door.

Once she was buckled in the passenger side of his truck, she looked around. "It's almost weird not to have Ben or Grant out here. I hope—" She bit the words off.

"Hope?"

She sighed. "Nothing."

"Can't shake that bad feeling, can you?"

"No. I can't."

He frowned. "Well, let's see what Baldwin has to say before you put any stock into it. After his interview, you might feel better."

"I might."

But for some reason, she didn't think so.

Mac sat next to Isabelle on one side of the two-way mirror. He could hear and see into the room on the other side of it, but anyone in the room wouldn't know he or Isabelle was there watching.

Drew Baldwin sat at the lone table in the middle of the room. He wore the orange prison jumpsuit and kept his eyes on his hands, which were cuffed in front of him.

Creed, carrying a manila folder, stepped into the room along with a professionally dressed woman who looked to be in her early thirties. She sat next to Baldwin, who shot her a scowl. "Who's she?"

"I know you've said you don't want representation, but Ms. Callahan has agreed to provide it should you wish to retain her. I also need to tell you that these proceedings are being recorded."

"Told you. I don't need a lawyer because I haven't done anything wrong." He lifted his hands to his mouth and gnawed on an already shredded nail. His leg jiggled under the table, and his eyes darted to the door, then back to Creed.

The sheriff sighed. "Drew, look, you're barely twenty years old. You're probably scared, but thinking you'll get out of this if you hold out long enough." He leaned forward. "News flash, kid. You're not getting out of this. We take attempted murder very seriously."

Drew slapped his hands to the table with a thud. The lawyer flinched and edged away from him. Creed simply moved closer and shot him a glare. Drew scowled right back. "How many times do I have to tell you people that I never tried to kill anyone?"

Creed opened the folder and slid a photo across the table to Drew. "This is a picture of a car that almost mowed down Isabelle Trent. One of my deputies was clipped by the mirror. Not too long before all that happened, you almost hit a woman in the crosswalk with your motorcycle. Watching the footage, it's obvious the driver of this car meant to hit one, or both, of those ladies—in the crosswalk. The driver never stepped on the brakes. Are you telling me that's a coincidence?"

"No. I mean yes. I mean…" He slapped a hand to his head.

"That's attempted murder in my book, kid."

"But I'm not in that car! Where would I get a car like that anyway? All you gotta do is run the plates and you'll see it doesn't belong to me."

"We ran the plates. It was stolen from a friend of mine. He just bought it two days ago. Stolen by someone wearing a black hoodie and black gloves. Sound familiar?"

"I'm telling you, it's not me. Can you get a look at the guy's face?"

"No, unfortunately, not a good one, anyway."

"Then look for my DNA in it. You won't find

it because I've never been in the car." He rubbed his hands down his face. "You found the car, right?"

"Yes, actually, we did. Right where you left it. Parked just outside of town on the side of the road. Probably where you left your bike."

"I didn't leave my bike anywhere!"

"You left it in the woods at the Trent ranch when you tried to burn the barn down."

"I wasn't trying to burn—"

The lawyer leaned forward. "I need to advise you not to say anything else until we've talked."

Drew shot her a baleful glance. "Shut up."

She sighed and sat back.

"And," Creed said, "we found the gasoline can you ditched near the barn and pulled a lighter out of your pocket when we searched you. We've got a piece of material that snagged on a branch that matches an article of your clothing. We've got a shoe print of the person who tried to snatch the baby—and seeing as how you've been camping out with the homeless under the bridge outside of town, I'm assuming you're wearing the only pair of shoes you have—and we now have impressions to compare. We've got you cold, Baldwin. Why don't you just come clean?"

The young man chewed off another fingernail and moved on to the one beside it. "I'll admit to the stuff I did," he finally said, dropping his hands to the table, "but I didn't steal that car and I didn't try to kill anyone." He crossed his arms and met Creed's stare over the table.

Isabelle sighed and leaned forward in the chair to massage her temples. "What do you think, Mac?"

"I think he's lying. He knows he's in big trouble. Copping to the little stuff will get him less time."

"Maybe."

He took her hand. "Isabelle, you're safe. The kids are coming home today. Enjoy it."

She smiled at him, but it wasn't hard to see she had to force it. "I think I'm ready to leave now. I have a lot to do before tomorrow."

"We."

"What?"

"*We* have a lot to do before tomorrow."

This time her lips curved in a genuine smile. "Yes. Yes, *we* do. Why don't we go join Cody Ray and Ms. Sybil? The other volunteers should be arriving soon, as well."

"Other former foster kids?"

"Yes."

"I look forward to meeting them."

Isabelle opened her mouth to say something, then snapped it shut. He wanted to know what she'd planned to say but decided maybe it was better if he didn't. Their conversation about him leaving and that kiss they'd shared was definitely the elephant in the room, but neither of them wanted to address it. Not now. They rode to the ranch in silence and when he pulled into the drive, the kids were home. "They're early," she said, the pure joy in her voice hitting Mac right in the heart. Isabelle jumped out of the truck.

"Izzy-belle! Mr. Mac!" Katie screeched her happiness and ran at them. Isabelle opened her arms and caught the little girl up in a tight hug. Even the boys ran to her and wrapped their arms around her.

Then Katie wiggled away from Isabelle and threw herself at Mac. Heart thudding, he lifted her to kiss her nose. She giggled and returned the gesture. Mac wanted to sit down and cry. How could he leave?

How could he not?

Katie caught his cheeks in her small hands. "We're back, Mr. Mac."

He cleared his throat. "And I'm so glad you are."

"Me, too. Will you take me fishing?"

Mac blinked. "Fishing? Where did that come from?"

She shrugged. "I watched a movie and it looked fun."

"Well, okay—" He stopped. He wasn't going to be here much longer, and he didn't need to make promises he wasn't going to keep.

"Katie," Isabelle said, "Why don't you go check on Lilly? I'm sure she's missed you."

"Okay! I've missed her, too."

Mac set her down and she scampered off toward the house. He looked at Isabelle. "Thanks."

She nodded and looked away, but not before he saw the sheen of tears in her eyes. Feeling like the lowest of the low, he turned to the boys. "Hi, guys, glad you're back."

"Us, too," Zeb said. He turned to Isabelle. "Ms. Cheryl came and got us at school and said you needed to see us."

"Well, she was right about that."

"We were glad," Donny said, "Cuz we needed to see you, too." He gave her another hug, then glanced at the house. "Something smells good. Did Ms. Sybil make cookies?"

"Of course. And a big batch of her rolls."

"Rolls! See ya!" He darted off, catching up with Katie on the front porch. He scooped her up, making her laugh, then the two disappeared inside.

Isabelle held Mac's gaze and he thought she might be silently asking him how he could leave.

The sound of an engine caught their attention,

once again rescuing him from his thoughts and her...sad resignation.

The police cruiser pulled to a stop and Ben climbed out to walk over to them. "I see the kids made it home."

"Yes," Isabelle said, a smile curving her lips but not quite reaching her eyes.

Mac didn't like the look on the deputy's face. "What is it?"

Ben shrugged. "Nothing major. I just thought I'd come see if there was anything I could do to help out for tomorrow."

Isabelle gave the man a brilliant grin. "Just ask Mac what he needs. I'm going to head on into the house and hug the kids one more time."

"You just want cookies," Mac said.

"I wouldn't turn them down." She winked and spun to hurry away.

When she was out of earshot, Mac turned to Ben. "Okay, spill it. Something going on with Baldwin?"

"I'm not sure." Ben leaned against his car and crossed his ankles. "The whole time he was talking, I kept thinking that I believe him."

"Why?"

"Because what he says makes sense. I'm not saying the kid isn't trouble, but I don't think he's a killer. And the timing of the almost hit-and-run doesn't add up. We have him on security footage on his bike looking through the window of the café where Isabelle was meeting with Travis, Regina and Donna. We also show him riding out of town. An hour later, the car tries to run down Isabelle and Regina."

"Sounds like the timing would work just fine for him to ditch his bike and steal the car."

"No, don't think so. At least not from the location it was reported stolen. I tried the route and timed it. It would have taken him at least thirty more minutes at the very least."

Mac crossed his arms, not liking the direction of the conversation. "Creed said the car was stolen from a friend of his. Whose was it?"

"Travis Lovett. Apparently, he had a big sale last week and kept it secret but went right out and bought the car for Valerie. He was in the meeting with Isabelle when Valerie called and reported it stolen. Said someone took it right out of the driveway. She'd left the keys in it to run back inside to get her phone and came back to find it gone."

"Could have still been Baldwin."

Ben nodded. "Could have. But the boot print on the fence didn't match his shoes."

"No?" That was interesting.

"No. And that's the only pair of shoes he's got on him. Nothing in his backpack or in the storage container on his bike."

Mac frowned. "So, what are you saying, Ben?"

"I'm saying things don't add up for me. And Creed is looking real hard at everything, too. He's going back and investigating everything from the beginning."

"I see." Actually, he didn't. "So if it's not Baldwin, why would someone be trying to hurt Isabelle?"

"I don't know, but let's keep this under our hats until tomorrow is finished. No need to stress her out any more than she already is with everything going on. Grant will be here and so will Creed and myself. Nothing's going to happen tomorrow to ruin that day as long as we can help it."

"I'm right there with you."

SEVENTEEN

Saturday morning dawned overcast and rainy, but the weather app said it should clear up in the next hour. Isabelle was praying it was right. She'd been eyeing the weather for the past week and so far, it hadn't changed its prediction for the day. As she fed the baby, she sent up silent prayers for the sun to come out.

Ms. Sybil stepped into the kitchen and brushed her hands over the apron. "It's going to get busy pretty quickly around here. You ready?"

"I'm ready. Cody Ray and Mac are getting everything set up. The other volunteers are on the way and already know what to do, Donna's already delivered the pastries, the cotton candy machine is here, Evie is on her way with the K-9, the kids' bowling alley is ready along with the other games. The ponies are in the smaller pasture for rides, the pig is greased, the dunking booth is set up, the dogs are put up, and the plastic bull is in the larger pasture for the kids to rope." She drew in a breath. "Have I forgotten anything?"

"I don't think so."

Ms. Sybil handed Lilly the bottle and the child grabbed it with both hands and stuck it in her mouth. "She's gotten the hang of doing that for herself."

"Yep, she's a good eater." She stood. "All right, I'm going to change and get ready to get this thing going." She paused. "Do I dare look out the window to check the weather?"

Ms. Sybil didn't have any hesitation. She looked, then laughed. "The Lord is good. The sun is shining and not a cloud in sight."

"Oh, thank you," Isabelle breathed. Then hurried to finish up all of the last-minute details needed to make sure it was a fun and profitable day for all.

When she stepped outside thirty minutes later, the volunteers had arrived. With tears in her eyes, Isabelle hugged each one. They kept in touch, but seeing them whole and happy never failed to warm her heart.

After they went to their respective stations and the people started arriving, Isabelle threw herself into the hostess's role and flitted from one group to the next.

She knew the town looked forward to this

day each year and she took pleasure in being able to provide it.

"Iz?"

She turned to see her father walking toward her, Lilly in his arms. "Dad!" She hurried to him and hugged him. "What are you doing here? Is Mom okay?"

"She's fine. Since your Aunt Tammy's here and is with her, I decided to ride over." She noticed his golf cart parked next to hers. "I saw Sybil had her hands full," he said, "so offered to take this little scamp and entertain her for a few minutes."

"She's a joy."

He shifted the baby to the other arm. "Haven't seen much of you lately."

"And you were a little worried so decided to put in an appearance?"

He smiled. "Something like that, but you know I love this day as much as you do."

"I know." He'd wanted to come see everyone and revel in the organized chaos. He'd also pitch in if he saw something that needed doing.

"I've been hearing rumors, so wanted to come hear from you what's going on."

The small-town gossip mill at work. She sighed. "It's been kind of exciting around here." She told him about Drew Baldwin but left out most of the scary details.

Her father frowned. "Saw his picture at the pharmacy, then spotted him a couple of days ago in the grocery store. I called Creed and let him know, but the guy was gone by the time a deputy showed up."

"Wait, what? When was this?" Isabelle asked.

"Ah, I don't know. Two days ago? Maybe three? Why?"

"Just wondering. Could it have been Tuesday midmorning?"

His frown deepened. "Yeah, suppose it could have been."

"Huh."

"What?"

"It might be nothing." Or it might be something. If Drew had been in the grocery store at the time she and Regina had been dodging the car in the crosswalk, then who had been driving?

Mac couldn't relax. From a distance, he kept an eye on things, but there were so many people that it was hard to keep track of Isabelle. And that made him nervous. Then again, there were reasonable arguments to be made that could implicate Baldwin in every single incident. He could have parked his bike on the side of the road, walked to the Lovett home, stolen the car, then come back to get his bike. He agreed with

Ben that the timeline was a bit questionable, but it still could have happened. Maybe.

"Hey, there."

He turned to find Isabelle behind him. "Those are some deep thoughts," she said. "Wanna share?"

"Everyone's having a good time. You've really done a wonderful job."

"I couldn't have done it without a lot of help. But yes, it's turning out to be pretty amazing. My stress level has gone down several notches."

And he didn't want to raise it again by telling her what Ben had said.

"When are you leaving?" she asked.

"After everyone is gone."

"I see."

He turned to her, his heart aching. "Isabelle—"

"Don't draw it out," she said. "Just go."

"I don't know if I can. You might still be in danger."

She froze.

So much for not adding back to her stress level. He explained what Ben had told him and that Creed was going back over every bit of the case against Baldwin.

"It doesn't matter," she said. "If you need to go, you need to go."

He gave a short laugh. "I'm not going if you're still in danger."

"I have very capable friends who happen to be in law enforcement. They'll take care of me. If you're leaving, you need to do so."

"But I—"

"Stop it! Don't delay it. You'll just break my heart even more. So, after everyone is gone, say your goodbyes to the kids and...go. Please." She turned on her heel and walked away. From behind, Mac saw her lift a hand and swipe it across her cheek.

He'd made her cry. His own throat closed, but he did as she said. He made the rounds. Speaking to the kids and telling them how they were special and he was glad they were back.

When he got to Katie, he almost couldn't speak. The little girl had wormed her way into his heart and he could feel it splintering. "Hey, Katie-girl, I need to say goodbye."

She frowned. "Where ya going?"

"I...just have to go away for a while. I have to go build a house."

"But...this is your home. Why you want to live somewhere else? How will I hug you if you go away?"

Mac didn't think he was going to be able to speak. This was what he'd been avoiding. Getting involved. Attaching his heart to others. Obviously, he'd failed. Miserably. Once he was gone, everything would be okay again.

"I'll take a hug now?"

"Okay." She held up her arms. Mac picked her up and buried his face in her sweet curls. Oh, this little girl. How had she managed to breach his defenses so easily? He didn't know the story of how she'd come to be with Isabelle, but he sent up a silent prayer for her safety.

Mac set her back on the ground. "You're a great kid, Katie. You're funny and smart and can be anything you want to be when you grow up. You remember that, okay?"

"Okay, Mr. Mac. And you're big as a mountain and you don't hit little girls and you have a very nice smile. And I love you. You remember that, too, okay?"

Mac was ready to lose it. He nodded, gave her one more hug and turned to find Isabelle watching them, tears shimmering in her eyes. He couldn't do it.

He walked over to her. "I'm not going."

"Yes, you are."

"What?"

"You're emotional right now. You've come to care about these kids and the rest of us. Don't make the decision to stay based on how you feel right now. Take some time. Figure out what it is that you really want. If you stay here, you won't have the distance to do that. And I think you need to call your family."

He did, but that was beside the point. "I can't leave with you still in possible danger."

"And if I wasn't in danger?"

He opened his mouth. Shut it. Isabelle nodded and squeezed his hand. "Exactly. Go. Figure out what you want."

He noticed she didn't say that she'd be waiting if he decided to come back.

Ben walked up to them, phone pressed to his ear. He held up a finger. "Well, looks like that's that."

Isabelle raised a brow. "What's what?"

"That was Creed. He left a while ago when he got a call that Baldwin wanted to talk to him. When Creed got there, Baldwin confessed to everything. Said he didn't want to go down for attempted murder, though. Said none of the incidents were supposed to kill anyone, just scare them. He said all of the incidents were just supposed to be distractions and he was hoping one would allow him to grab Lilly and run with her."

"But that doesn't make any sense," Isabelle said. "She wasn't even with me at the café when the car came at Regina and me."

Ben shrugged. "I dunno. He just said he did it and he was signing a confession. Creed is still talking to him, but it looks like you're safe and sound now."

"I see." She looked at Mac. "I guess that means you can go with a clear conscience now."

"Isabelle—"

But he was talking to her back. He dug a foot into the dirt, then kicked a rock. It bounced off his truck and he sighed.

It really was time for him to go.

EIGHTEEN

Once again, Isabelle couldn't sleep, so she paced. From the den to the kitchen, to the kids' rooms…to Mac's door. Knowing the space behind it was empty cramped her heart in a way that she hadn't felt in a long time. It was a different kind of pain than the one she'd experienced when Josiah died, but it was still pain.

And she couldn't get away from it.

The way she'd walked away from Mac earlier gnawed at her. That had been wrong. She'd let her hurt overtake her and she'd reacted. With a sigh, she sent him a text.

I'm sorry. I shouldn't have let you leave without saying goodbye. Know that I'm praying you're able to work things out to your satisfaction. You're a wonderful man, Mac, and I'm grateful for everything you did while you were here.

She waited to see if he'd respond. When, in the next few minutes, she didn't get the three little dots, she set the phone aside and pinched the bridge of her nose. She had to do something. Pacing and thinking were just making her bonkers. She turned and walked into the den to pick up the toys still scattered on the floor. She picked up one of Katie's pretend cupcakes and smiled at the memory of her bringing the one to Mac and him stuffing it in his mouth.

Tears rose once more.

Lord, You know best. I truly believe that. Just help me understand how having Mac leave is the best thing for anyone. Because right now, I don't see it.

A noise outside the French doors lifted her head and she stiffened. Cody Ray had left shortly after they'd finished cleaning up, to spend the night with his brother's family before heading to the beach for a few days of well-deserved rest.

Ms. Sybil had opted to go along, after Isabelle's urging.

Drew Baldwin had confessed to everything. She was fine. The kids were safe. She continued her cleaning and had started toward her bedroom when another noise near the kitchen window had her pulse pounding faster and her palms sweating. "It's nothing," she whispered. "It's just—"

In the kitchen, the sound of glass breaking pulled a gasp from her. Not again. And she'd left her cell phone on the counter. Had Drew somehow managed to get out of custody? Surely someone would have called. And she hadn't bothered to set the alarm because she was still up and everyone was supposed to be safe.

Isabelle raced to the boys' room and shook Danny's shoulder. He groaned and opened his eyes. "Get up, Danny," she whispered. "Someone's trying to get in and I left my cell phone in the kitchen. Do you have yours?"

"Yes." Sleep fled from his eyes.

"Good. Good. Can you give it to me?"

He snatched it off the end table and handed it to her. She punched in 911. It rang. "Get Zeb and go out the window," she told the boy. "Don't worry about the screen, just push it out. Break it if you have to. You understand?"

"Yes, ma'am." He rolled out of bed to pull on his slippers.

"Hurry, Danny, I'm going to get Katie and pass her out to you and Zeb," Isabelle whispered. Dispatch picked it up.

She left him waking Zeb and hurried to peer around the doorjamb while the woman on the other end of the line asked what her emergency was. But Isabelle didn't dare speak. She just prayed the woman could track the call.

Isabelle turned the volume of the phone down low. She couldn't take a chance her voice could be heard by whoever was in her house. The hallway was empty. She darted into Katie's room and hurried to the child's side. She touched her shoulder. "Katie, wake up, baby. I need you to go with Zeb and Danny."

"Ma'am?" the dispatcher's voice reached her. "Can you talk to me?"

"Someone's breaking into my house." Isabelle rattled off her address. "I'm getting the children out. Track my location if you can."

"How many children?"

"Four. Katie? Come on, honey, wake up."

"What's wrong, Izzy-belle?" The little girl yawned, then frowned. "I don't want to get up yet."

Before Isabelle could answer, she heard more noises from the kitchen. Her heart pounded in her throat. "I'm going to put you out your window. Danny and Zeb are waiting for you."

"But—"

"Shh." Isabelle covered the child's mouth with a finger. "Act like you're playing hide-and-seek, okay? Only you and the boys and Lilly are all going to hide together and be as quiet as you can be."

Some of Isabelle's desperation and fear must have reached the child's subconscious, because her eyes widened and she nodded. "Okay. I'm good at hiding when the bad man's around."

Her words broke Isabelle's heart as she helped the little girl out of her window. Zeb knelt and Katie climbed on his back.

"I'm going to get Lilly," Isabelle whispered. "Go to her window."

Isabelle checked the hallway once again just in time to see a figure enter her bedroom. *Oh, God, please keep us safe.*

It wouldn't take him long to realize she wasn't in there. She bolted for Lilly. She took precious moments to carefully lift the sleeping baby, praying she wouldn't cry out. Lilly stirred, but simply buried her face in Isabelle's shoulder with a soft sigh.

A thump and a curse came from her room. She moved quickly, her mind racing, trying desperately to figure out who could be there. She went to the window, unlocked it and shoved the screen to the ground. She passed Lilly to Danny and he tucked the baby under his chin. "What are we doing?" he asked.

"Run to Poppa's house. Take the short cut through the trees. No matter what happens or what you hear, you don't stop. If we can get there, we can get help. Okay?" She handed him the phone. "Go, now. I'm coming."

The kids took off toward the woods and Isabelle swung a leg over the windowsill.

Something hard pressed into the back of her head and she froze. "You're not going anywhere except with me."

Mac drove with one hand on the wheel. He was an idiot. If they gave out awards for biggest idiot of the year—no, the century—he'd win first place. Hands down, no doubt about it. Actually, he was worse than an idiot. He was a coward.

He shouldn't have left. They might be safe—and he was very glad of it—but the realization that it was hurting him far more to leave behind the people he'd come to love in such a short time than it would if he'd just stayed put, left him reeling.

How?

Again, the mental picture of his house on the hill came to mind. And with it, the emptiness. Empty table, empty rooms, empty life—empty heart.

Will you take me fishing?

How can I hug you if you're not here?

I'm glad you came to the ranch, Mr. Mac.

Ms. Isabelle smiles more. And that's saying a lot cuz she smiles all the time.

He slammed on brakes and pulled to the shoulder of the road and dialed his sister's number. When he got her voice mail, he said, "I'm sorry, Nancy. I'm an idiot. I know that's not news, but at least you know that I'm willing to acknowledge it. I want to see you. I want to meet my niece. I'm sorry it's taken me so long to come to my senses. I hope you can forgive me. If I don't answer when you call me back, I'm not ignoring you. I just have something that I have to take care of and it may take a while. But I love you and I'll see you soon." He hung up, his heart beating fast, but a joy in knowing he was doing the right thing flowing through him.

The right thing with his family, anyway, but what about Isabelle?

Why was he leaving when everything in him wanted to stay?

The absurdity of it had him spinning the wheel into a U-turn. He wasn't leaving. He was going back to beg Isabelle's—and the children's—forgiveness and ask for his job back. Then he planned to ask Isabelle out on a date. Assuming she was good with the first part of the plan.

Please let her be good with the first part of the plan.

His phone rang and he didn't recognize the number. He activated his Bluetooth. "Hello?"

"Isabelle's in trouble, Mr. Mac. A man broke into the house and took her."

Danny's frantic words sent his heart racing. "Where are you? The other kids?"

"At her parents' house. I called 911 and they're looking for her, but I think he's going to hurt her."

"Who was it? Who took her?"

"I don't know." Danny paused. "He sounded kind of familiar, but I don't know who he reminded me of."

"Think hard, Danny. I'm on my way."

"I have to go now." The boy's voice lowered. "Bye." The call disconnected and Mac pressed the gas while prayers left his lips one after the other.

He voice-dialed Creed's number and the man answered with a gruff, "What?"

"Did Baldwin escape your custody?"

"No. But I just listened to the 911 call and am on the way to Isabelle's parents' place. About a minute away. How'd you know she was in trouble?"

"Danny called me just before I called you. I'm on my way to the ranch."

"There's no one there. Isabelle's father already went over and called me."

Mac's heart nosedived. "Who took her, Creed?"

"I have no idea."

Isabelle still didn't know who her abductor was as he kept his voice in a low whisper, a quiet hiss that sent shivers up her spine and dread into her heart. When he'd placed the gun against her head, she'd frozen for a split second, then quickly obeyed him and stepped back into the room.

Desperate to buy time for the kids to get away, she'd held her hands up and faced him, praying he wouldn't shoot her and then go after the children. "What do you want?" She kept her voice low, hoping that by staying calm, she could gain an upper hand somehow.

"Your cooperation. As long as I have that, I won't have to hurt the kids."

"Who are you?"

"Walk out the front door and keep going," he'd said. "To the tree line and down the path."

Isabelle had thought that maybe it was better she didn't know who he was. As long as he was wearing a mask and she didn't know him, maybe he'd let her go. But what did he *want*?

She'd followed his instructions and walked out the door. He'd prodded her with the weapon at her back to the tree line. Now, with the house behind her and the wooded area in front of her, she shivered in the night air and wished she'd grabbed a coat. "Where are we going?"

"My truck."

Isabelle walked the path that had been made before she'd taken over the property. It struck her that her captor knew about it. He'd guided her to it with no hesitation. How? From watching her? Or because he knew her and her property?

Again, his voice sounded familiar, but he'd kept it so low and raspy she couldn't put her finger on it. Praying the children had made it safely to her parents, she pushed on.

"Here," he said. "Through those limbs where I hid the truck."

She froze. *That* voice she knew. She whirled. "Travis?"

He muttered a curse and ripped the mask from his face. Isabelle stared, her heart thudding in her throat. She didn't know whether to be even more afraid or relieved. Surely Travis, whatever he was doing, wouldn't hurt her? "What's going on?"

"Because it's time to end this once and for all."

"End what? And please, put the gun down. You don't need it."

He lifted it slightly so that it pointed at her head instead of her heart. His eyes glittered in the half-moon light. Cold. Empty. Desperate. Determined.

The fear returned tenfold. "What are you doing?" she whispered.

"Let's not drag this out," he said. "I need your land and you're going to sell it to me. Tonight."

"But…what? Why?"

"Because if you don't, I'm going to wind up bankrupt and I can't let that happen. I already have a buyer for this place."

"You already have—" Isabelle snapped her lips shut. *Get it together, Isabelle.* "What? But you just bought Valerie a new car."

"With the earnest money the buyer sent for this land. I know she was thinking about leaving me and I can't let her do that. I can afford a divorce even less than I can afford my family."

Leaving him? "Valerie never said a word about leaving you, Travis. She was only supportive. And earnest money? It's not your land to sell!"

"It will be. Now move. Into the truck."

She pushed the shock away and focused on what she had to do to survive. "Travis. I don't think you've thought this through. If I disappear, and you show up with the deed to the land, don't you think that's going to look a little suspicious?"

"I've already worked it out. No need to worry

yourself about that." He jabbed her with the gun. "In the truck."

Did she have a choice? If she took off running, would he really shoot her? When still she hesitated, he sighed. "Isabelle, I'm tired. Tired of waiting for you to come to your senses and take me up on my very generous offer, tired of Valerie harping about money, tired of my brats always needing something. I'm tired of working all the time to finally have a little money in the bank and then having to spend it on a home repair, a doctor bill, or whatever." He clenched his teeth and she thought he might pull the trigger right there, but he drew in a breath. "I don't want to involve those foster kids of yours, but if you don't cooperate, they'll suffer. I know you sent them running and I know they probably went straight to your parents' place. So I know where to find them. And you parents."

At his tone, her heart chilled. He totally meant the horrendous words. Isabelle opened the passenger door and slid into the seat. "What now?"

"Hold out your hands." She did so, and with one hand aiming the weapon at her, he reached with the other into his pocket and pulled out a zip tie. "Link your fingers and slide your hands through."

Isabelle wanted to refuse, but the picture of her sweet kids at the mercy of this man made her swallow hard. She obeyed, clasped her fingers and kept them stiff so her palms were slightly separated. She prayed he wouldn't notice. He pulled the tie tight then handed her the seat belt buckle. "Buckle up." She stared at him, sighed, then pulled the strap across and fastened the device. He slammed the door.

She considered making a run for it once more, but again, the thought of him making good on his threat to hurt the children or her parents stilled her. Besides, she'd never be able to get the seat belt back off and open the door before he—

He climbed into the driver's side, shut the door and looked at her. "It's nothing personal, Isabelle."

"Funny, it feels pretty personal to me."

He scowled and cranked the old truck she knew he only used for his home like hauling mulch or moving furniture.

"Tell me how you plan to get away with this," she said. "You owe me that at least."

"I don't suppose it will hurt. When you were talking about the trouble the baby's father was causing, I decided to piggyback on it and use him as the fall guy. Then Donna said he almost ran her down in the crosswalk, so I thought if I did the same, the police would connect the two. It was working perfectly until he got caught."

Isabelle listened, her jaw tightening against

the words she wanted to hurl at him. "I thought you were my friend," she whispered. She'd had no inkling of the darkness in him. How had she been so blind to that? "How do you think you're going to get away with this?" She couldn't fathom it.

"You're in trouble financially," he said. "Everyone knows you need the money from the fundraiser to stay afloat. If you were to lose that, you'd go under."

"We raised the money."

"Ah, but no one has to know that. All of those checks never have to reach the bank, do they?" He patted his pocket. "I knew they'd be in your desk just waiting to be deposited on Monday morning. All I have to do is say we had a deal."

"What kind of deal?" *Keep him talking.* It wouldn't be hard. He actually sounded quite proud of himself.

"I'd buy the land from you and let you live on it and keep running it, so that the kids would be able to stay in a secure home." He shrugged. "Only now that's impossible because you're gone and I don't need the land. My only option is to unload it."

"But people know they wrote checks. Surely, when they're not deposited, they'll wonder why?"

He shrugged. "That's something for the authorities to work on. By the time they figure it out—if they ever do—I'll be long gone."

"You're a monster," she whispered.

His hand fisted and for a moment she thought he might hit her. Then he spun the wheel onto a side road and took a deep breath. When he glanced back to her, his eyes had hardened to the point that she wondered if he even had a conscience anymore. "You're going to kill me, aren't you?"

"Like I said, it's nothing personal." He swallowed and looked away, giving her a slight hope that maybe she'd been wrong. Maybe she could reach him.

"It's not too late, Travis. You haven't hurt me. Just let me go and we can chalk this up to a bad choice with a happy ending."

He raked a hand through his hair. "Sorry, Isabelle, but I can't do that. I'm too far into this."

"I see. And if I don't sign over the property to you?"

He studied her. "You'll sign."

Chills skated up her spine and a sickness grew in her gut. "Why do you say that?"

"Because you love those kids and you don't want to see them get hurt." His icy gaze met hers once more as he braked for a curve. "And I will hurt them. One by one until you give me what I want. But truly, you and I both know it won't come to that."

He was right. She'd never let it go so far that he even came close to one of the kids. She pressed her bound hands to her head and silently prayed.

NINETEEN

Mac paced the porch of Isabelle's home. Creed must have friends in high places because he already had a crime scene unit going over the inside. The place felt empty. Abandoned. The horses were in the barn, the cows in the far pasture. Even the dogs were gone, traveling with Cody Ray and Ms. Sybil. Isabelle's absence was distinct, and his heart pounded with fear for her.

Creed stepped up beside him. "I don't know who could have taken her," he said, his voice soft but tense. "I literally don't have a clue."

"We need to talk to her friends. What about Regina?"

"She said she had no idea, either, but she's put a list of people together that talk to Isabelle on a regular basis and is going door-to-door to see if they know anything, while we try to find something here."

Mac pressed his hands to his eyes. "Drew

Baldwin confessed to trying to kill Isabelle, right?"

"He did."

"Obviously, he lied. Why? What makes a guy willing to take the hit for a murder he didn't have anything to do with?"

"I can only think of one thing," Creed said.

"Money?"

"Yep."

"Maybe we need to talk to Baldwin again," Mac said. "I hate to leave here, but I don't think she's coming back and I need to be doing something proactive like Regina."

Creed nodded. "I've already put a call out to the media and the news is running a special report that she's missing and asking for information, but I'm with you. Let's go talk to Baldwin once more. Want to ride with me?"

"Sure."

Mac followed the man to his cruiser and climbed into the passenger seat. His heart thudded and fear threatened to swallow him. Who wanted to hurt Isabelle so bad and why? Nothing made sense. *God, please don't let me lose her. I know she's not officially mine, but You and I both know I'm head over heels about her and I really need her to be okay. Please, God, let us find her so I can be honest about how I feel. And yes, I realize that might be a totally selfish prayer, but just...please...*

Creed slid behind wheel and radioed his deputies to let them know what he was doing. Just as he cranked the SUV, his phone rang. He answered it with the Bluetooth. "Creed Payne."

"Creed? It's Regina. I've been talking to Valerie Lovett about Isabelle and I think you need to hear what she has to say. Can you meet us at the station?"

"I'm on the way there now to talk to Drew Baldwin."

"We'll see you there."

Ten minutes later, Creed wheeled the vehicle into the designated parking spot and Mac followed him into the station.

Regina met them at the door. "I put her in the conference room. She said she had some information that might help us find Isabelle."

"She tell you what it was?"

"No. She said she needed to tell you."

He frowned and nodded. "All right. Mac, you can listen in behind the mirror."

"Thanks." Mac made his way to the area he'd shared with Isabelle the last time he'd been at the station. Impatience clawed at him. He didn't want to be in the station; he needed to be searching for Isabelle.

His fingers rolled into fists as he stepped up

to the window to see Valerie Lovett seated at the table, her fingers twisted around a manila folder.

Creed walked into the room and tears formed in her eyes to spill over her lashes. The sheriff went to her and pulled her into his arms. "Aw, Val, come on, now. It'll be all right."

She nodded against his shoulder, sniffed and swiped her eyes. He handed her a tissue from the box and she drew in a deep breath. "I need to tell you something, but I don't know how to do it. Everyone's going to hate me." She stifled a sob on the last word. But instead of breaking down again, she firmed her jaw and looked Creed in the eye. "I lied, Creed."

"About?" Creed settled into the chair across from her.

"About the car. Travis and I have been having some issues and I've been very angry with him about a lot of things. But this time—"

"Go on," he said when she stopped.

"I don't know where Isabelle is, but I think Travis had something to do with her disappearance."

Creed straightened, and Mac's heart pounded harder.

"What do you mean?"

"Travis said he sold the Cooper Hill house over on Highway 21. He said he used that to buy me the little red sports car. Which is stupid because I've never wanted anything like that, nor asked for it, but he was so happy about it that I did my best to thank him and be thrilled that he wanted to spoil me like that. But then he drove it to the restaurant to meet Isabelle and the others that morning when they were going to talk about the Day at the Ranch details. A short time later, he texted and said the that the car had been stolen, but he didn't want anyone to know it had been stolen from *him*. He said it would be better for insurance purposes if I told them the car had been stolen out of the driveway." She rubbed her eyes. "Honestly, I didn't see what the difference was. I mean if the car was stolen, it was stolen, but he said he had his reasons. However, I didn't feel right about lying."

"But you did."

"Yes." She sighed. "I did. He told me what to say and I called the station and said it. Later, when I learned the car had been used in the hit-and-run, I nearly had a stroke."

"So, why didn't you come forward then?"

Her chin wobbled before she got it under control. "I confronted Travis about it and he told me to leave it alone, that if I pressed him or changed my story, he'd be out a ton of money and we would be in major trouble. I didn't understand, but obviously, I knew something wasn't right." She pressed her lips together, then said, "I kept thinking and thinking about it and I couldn't get the thought out of my head that the car had been awfully easy to find. I mean, who steals that kind of car and just leaves it on the side of the road in perfect condition? And then I had the thought of what if—"

She pressed her fingers to her eyes. "Go ahead, Valerie. What if—"

Valerie swallowed and Mac wanted to shake whatever she was trying to say out of her. But that wouldn't help the situation.

"I woke up tonight to see Travis slip out of the house," she said. "I couldn't leave the kids to follow him, but I called my parents and told them I was having an emergency and I needed them to come stay the rest of the night. I wanted to see what he was up to. When I couldn't find him, I came home and went through his office, hoping there would be something that would tell me what was going on with him."

What did all of this have to do with Isabelle? It was all Mac could do not to burst into the room and demand she get to the point.

"Answer me this, first. You say you don't know where Isabelle is," Creed said.

"No, I don't."

"Then I'm confused."

"I know. I'm getting there." She slid the manila envelope across the table. "I think Travis may be trying to force Isabelle to sell her property to him."

Mac flinched and Creed jerked. "Force her?" he asked. "How so?"

"By scaring her into selling, maybe? I'm not sure. I have a hard time believing he'd hurt her, but... I just don't know and that means I can't keep silent." She nodded to the folder. "Everything's in there. I made copies in case I needed them later, but then Regina showed up and—" She waved a hand. "There's a contract on the property with a condominium developer and a copy of a check from that developer for a hundred thousand dollars of earnest money."

Creed ran a hand down his face. "Where's Travis now?"

"I don't know, but when Regina said Isabelle was missing, my first thought was this. He's in this too deep to have it fall through. If this deal doesn't happen then he's finished."

"Which makes him desperate," Mac whispered.

About five miles outside of the town limits, Travis made a sudden turn onto a dirt road between towering trees, and Isabelle tensed even more. This was it. This was where he was taking her. Nausea swirled in her gut and she had to swallow several times before she could speak. "Where are we?"

"A place where we can conduct our business without worrying about interruption."

The winding road led through the thick wooded area and finally opened up into a small clearing just big enough to hold a small log-cabin-style home. "Whose house is this?"

"No one's right now." He pulled in front of the cabin and parked. "Stay put." She obeyed, watching him and surveying the area at the same time. He climbed out of the driver's seat and walked around to open her door. "Get out."

It took three tries with her bound—and almost numb—hands, but finally, Isabelle unhooked the seat belt and hauled herself out of the seat. With dread, she realized he'd chosen the location well. Even if she could get away from him and run, where would she go? She could walk the five or six miles back to town with no trouble, but the only problem was, he'd know that was exactly where she'd head and would know the route she'd take.

He put a hand on her back and shoved her toward the door. "Stand to the side." She did so while he used his phone to unlock the lockbox.

"This is one of your listings, isn't it?"

He glanced at her. "Yeah."

He twisted the knob and Isabelle lifted her

bound hands then brought them down on the side of his head. He cried out as the momentum of her hit sent him slamming into the partially opened door. Isabelle bolted down the porch steps and darted toward the trees. Even as she ran, she knew it was a hopeless attempt, but she had to try. She needed to try. She knew her parents and the kids—and Mac—would all want her to try.

She dodged limbs and trunks and undergrowth, her feet churning, slipping every so often, but somehow, she managed to keep her balance.

"Isabelle! Stop! There's nowhere for you to hide!"

She kept going, breathing hard, looking for a place she could hunker down until he gave up.

Her foot caught on something and she went down hard. A cry slipped from her, then her head bounced against a solid object. Stars danced before her eyes and she lay there panting, blinking, mentally ordering herself to get up.

Travis's footsteps crashed closer and she was out of time. She shut her eyes and forced herself to go limp. He nudged her with a foot and she flopped over onto her back.

When his hand touched the wound on her

forehead, she refused to react. "Great," he muttered, "just great."

How long could she pretend to be knocked out before he became suspicious?

With a grunt, he hefted her into a fireman's carry. She hung facedown over his shoulder and couldn't stop the grimace at the pressure the position put on her pounding head. But she bit her lip and stayed as loose as possible.

"You're going to pay for this one, Isabelle," he muttered. "Trust me, you're going to pay."

TWENTY

Mac raked a hand through his hair for the umpteenth time. He'd be surprised if he had any left by the time they found Isabelle. And they would find her. There was no other option.

"Where would Travis take her if he's the one behind this?" Creed asked.

Valerie shook her head. "I don't know. I mean, I guess he could take her to a hotel or something. We have a beach house, but my parents are using it this week."

Her phone beeped once more from the recesses of her purse, and again, she ignored it.

"Can you call to make sure? While you do that, I'm going to take care of another matter."

She nodded and Creed walked out of the room. Mac met him in the hallway. "What do you think?"

"I think I want to talk to Baldwin and see if he can tell us where Travis might take Isabelle." His phone buzzed and he glanced at the screen, then looked up with a tight smile. "That's Ben. I sent him to get a warrant signed by the judge in Asheville to let us pull Baldwin's financial records. He just got back and is working on pulling the files. We should have that shortly."

"Excellent." Timber Creek might be a small town, but Creed knew his stuff and Mac was relieved he was in charge of Isabelle's disappearance.

"Hang tight. We're going to find her."

"I know."

Mac returned to the viewing room and paced the floor. As soon as Drew Baldwin was led into the room opposite the one Valerie was in, Mac simply turned his chair around to watch.

He could hear Valerie talking to her mother in the background.

Baldwin sat at the table, hands cuffed, nails bitten to the quick. "Okay, Drew," Creed said, leaning forward, "we know you changed your story and confessed that you were the one in the red car that tried to run down Isabelle. Why'd you lie?"

"What are you talking about?"

"We know it wasn't you in the car."

"How do you know that?"

"Because we know who was really driving. We also know you got a phone call at the jail. Who was it?"

Baldwin shrugged. "My mother."

"Your mother's dead."

The prisoner blinked, and Creed's lips tightened a fraction. "I'm not a stupid man, son. I didn't get this badge at a local yard sale. I know how to do my homework and I did it on you. Who was the call from?"

"I don't know. He didn't tell me his name."

"I see." Creed linked his hands together in front of him. "So you're saying a stranger called you up because he heard you were in jail and… what? What did he want?"

"Nothing." He shrugged.

Again, Mac was ready to burst through the mirror and throttle him. How much time were they wasting while Isabelle was in the hands of a man who'd already tried to kill her several times over. Was she okay? Was she even still alive? He swallowed and refused to allow his thought to go further down that path.

The door to the interrogation room opened and Regina stepped inside. "I got the phone records from the jail. The call that Mr. Baldwin took came in just after lunch, and was traced back to a burner phone, but the call pinged off the tower near downtown."

"Okay, thanks."

She switched papers. "Also, there was a deposit into the account of Mr. Drew Baldwin in the amount of twenty-five thousand dollars."

Drew sat up with an indrawn breath. "How'd you get that?"

"It's called a warrant," Creed said. "All nice and legal so we can send you away for quite a while. Unfortunately for you, we'll have to confiscate the money since it was used to buy your cooperation in a crime."

Baldwin shot to his feet. "You can't do that! That's my money!"

"Not anymore. Now sit down. I'm bigger and stronger than you are, and you'll lose if things get physical."

Drew stared at Creed for a few minutes, then sat. Mac admired the sheriff's calm way of dealing with the kid,

"Tell me about the money," Creed said.

Baldwin let out a sigh and dropped his chin to his chest. "He said he'd pay me the money," he finally said, his eyes on the table, "if I'd confess to the charges to give him some time, but then, after next week, I could say I didn't do it and they'd drop the charges."

"And you believed him?"

He shrugged. "I wanted the money."

Of course he did. "Come on, Creed," Mac muttered, "ask him where Isabelle is."

A buzzing sound came through the speakers and Mac turned back to see Valerie off the phone, but staring at her screen. She stood with a gasp.

Regina looked up and Mac focused his attention on the room behind him. "What is it?" Regina asked.

"A notification that someone used the lockbox on the house off Timber Mile Road. It's up the mountain and in a very secluded area. There are only about ten houses up there and they're mostly farm or ranching properties with a lot of acreage." Timber Creek had that small-town feel when one was on Main Street, but in reality, it covered a lot of land.

"Who has access to that lockbox?"

She bit her lip. "Just Travis and me."

"Hold on, let me get Creed." Regina left the room, appeared in the doorway of Baldwin's room and motioned to Creed. He followed her out and both of them entered Valerie's room.

"What's the address?" Creed asked.

She rattled it off to him and Mac tapped it into the maps app on his phone. Twenty-four minutes from the station. Up a winding mountain road. He walked out of the viewing room and headed for his truck—only to remember he'd ridden with Creed.

Mac spun on his heel to see Creed exiting the interview room with Regina and Valerie right behind him. "I assume you've already got the address programmed into your GPS?" Creed asked.

Mac waved the phone at him. "Can we please get going?"

Creed nodded. "Valerie sent me the floor plan of the home. You can look on the way. Regina, you put Valerie in the cell and stay with her. I hate to do it to her, but I've got to hold her."

"She knows. That's why she made arrangements for her kids before she agreed to come down here."

Sympathy for the woman who was just as much a victim as Isabelle pinged through Mac.

"Regina, tell Grant and Ben to meet us out there. Mac, come on."

He didn't have to say that twice.

Isabelle wasn't sure how long she could get away with pretending to be unconscious, but she would take advantage of it for as long as possible in order to give someone a chance to find her. The fact that she *knew* someone—probably Creed and Mac and every deputy on the force—was looking for her brought her great comfort. She just needed to stay alive long enough for one of them to find her. Her head pounded a fierce rhythm, and while she'd love a couple of ibuprofen pills, that was the least of her worries.

Footsteps drew closer and Travis nudged her with a toe. When she didn't respond, he whispered a curse and stomped away.

With her hands still bound in front of her—and growing more numb with each passing minute—Isabelle's hopes of escape dwindled quickly. She'd thought she'd kept enough space between her wrists when he'd pulled the zip tie tight, but even pressing her palms together, she couldn't loosen it enough to keep the blood flowing.

With her eyes cracked, she watched Travis pace in front of the kitchen doorway, muttering and raking his hand through his hair. He spun and walked to the table. He ruffled some papers, rearranged them, then muttered some more.

He spun to look at her and she slammed her eyes shut. "Come on, Isabelle, we both know you're faking."

She lay still, barely breathing, praying he didn't truly believe she was conscious. *He's just trying to call your bluff. Stay still, don't respond.*

When she didn't say anything or move, he returned to the kitchen. She heard him opening and closing drawers and cabinets and finally the water running.

Seconds later, when the wet rag hit her face, she couldn't help the gasp that escaped. She blinked and lifted her almost nonresponsive hands to swipe the water from her eyes.

"I knew it," Travis said. "Get up here to the table and let's get this done." He grasped her upper arm and pulled her to her feet. Weakness hit her, and she stumbled. Without his hand on her arm, she would've gone back to the floor.

He shoved her into the nearest chair and slapped a pen into her right hand. Her fingers wouldn't work properly, and it fell to the table. His cheeks darkened, his anger palpable. "Quit playing around with me," he said. "This isn't a game. I'm ready for this to be over with as much as you probably are."

"Not really," she said. "Having this over with for me means I'm dead."

He slammed a fist on the table and she jumped, but kept her gaze on his.

"Just sign it."

"I can't, Travis. My hands and fingers are numb. If you want me to use a pen, you're going to have to cut this off." She lifted her hands toward him.

He studied her for a brief moment as though he didn't believe her. Then picked up her hands and rubbed her fingers. She wanted to yank away from his touch but forced herself to remain still.

She needed her hands free.

He needed her signature.

She knew who would eventually win that battle.

With a growl, he reached into his pocket and pulled out a large switchblade hunting knife. He opened the blade and placed it between her hands, cutting through the plastic with one swipe. Her hands fell apart and she tried curling her fingers. At first they wouldn't cooperate, then slowly, she worked them until fire shot along her nerve endings, the feeling returning with a vengeance.

He set the knife on the table to his left and shoved the pen at her. "Here." His elbow knocked the open knife to the floor, but he ignored it, his attention focused on his greed, the papers and the pen. "Start signing."

"Can I at least read it while my hands return to normal? They're still burning."

He huffed a laugh and shook his head, eyes glittering. "They're closing documents."

"You're supposed to have a lawyer present to make this legal."

"I have one. You'd be amazed at what money can buy. Now read if you must, but you have two minutes."

Two minutes. Two minutes to figure out how to get away from this man.

Her eyes dropped to the floor. To the knife

near his chair. She thought he might have forgotten about it. He wanted those papers signed so badly that he was getting careless.

While she stared, she thought and flexed her fingers. She could sign her name now, but as soon as she did, she was dead. Unless…

She looked up. "You can't kill me in here. This place is for sale. What are you going to do to me after I sign the papers?"

"Just sign them! Do it or I'll tie you back up and go get one of those brats you care so much about and bring him back here! Trust me, you don't want me to do that."

He would and she'd wind up signing.

She blew out a shaky breath and nodded. "Calm down, Travis. I'll sign your papers." She picked up the pen. "No one's going to believe I'd willingly do this—especially not my parents."

"I guess we'll find out, won't we?"

"One more question before I sign."

"What?" He practically screamed the word.

"Will you please put my body somewhere it can be found? I don't want my parents—" or Mac "—wondering if I'm ever going to show back up."

He blinked and backed up a couple of steps. "Yes." He swallowed. "I'll do that."

"Thank you." Had she really just said *thank you*? She scribbled her name on the first page, then flipped it to the next. He held the gun and paced, keeping an eye on her, never quite turning his back.

Because the ranch was only in her name now, all he needed was her signature. She signed and flipped, trying to control her raging fear and ragged breathing. Her mind worked, frantic with each turn of the page. Her hand shook with each scribble of her name. *Please, God, help me. And be with Mac. Lord, if it's not to be for me to live much longer, please don't let Mac give up on living. Give him the peace he needs to find love again. To love himself again. To love You like he needs to.*

The next page she flipped off the table and to the floor. He sighed. "Pick it up."

Isabelle bent and snagged the paper, pulling it over the knife, hiding it. With her other hand, she grabbed the weapon and straightened.

Heart thundering in her chest, she wondered if he'd seen her. She set the paper on the stack with her left hand and slid the knife under her thigh with her right.

"Finish it," he said. "I need to get home before Valerie notices I'm gone."

No, he hadn't seen her. He was too focused on his greed and his desire for her signature on the papers. He had tunnel vision at the moment, and it was up to her to make that work in her favor. She picked up the pen once more and looked around. The place had been lightly staged with a few pieces of furniture strategically placed to make it more appealing to a potential buyer.

His eyes flicked to her once more. She signed the next page and turned it face down on the growing stack.

"Faster," he snapped.

With a flimsy plan in her head—and wondering if she could actually carry it out—she finished signing. When she turned the last piece of paper over, Travis let out a long sigh.

She kept her hand on the stack and set the pen on top of them. "Now what?"

He met her gaze. "I'm really sorry it came to this, Isabelle."

"Well, it hasn't actually come to anything yet. I'm still alive, which means there's still time to change your mind."

"And go to prison when you go to the police? I don't think so."

She nodded, not bothering to tell him she wouldn't go to the cops. They both knew she would. She gathered every ounce of courage she could muster. It was going to be either her or him. "Could you tell me how all of this even came about?"

He hesitated, then shrugged, seeming to relax

a fraction now that he had what he wanted. Good. She needed him to think he'd won, that she was beaten. "It was pretty simple," he said. "About six months ago, an investor was scouting places around here that would make a good tourist spot. He wants to build condos for a time-share company. He spotted your land and came into my office to talk to me about it."

"That sounds right. You came out to see me and asked if I'd ever thought about selling."

"You said no and while I was frustrated, I let it go."

"So what changed?"

"Last month, they came back, upped their offer substantially, so I started thinking how I could get you to move. I couldn't come up with anything believable until that day in the café."

"When I told you about someone causing all the trouble at the ranch."

"Yeah. Only I didn't have enough time to come up with a really good plan. It was an impulse shot when I jumped in the car and tried to run you down. I didn't even think much about it. And I failed." He rubbed a hand over his face. "But it all worked out in the end. That's all that matters."

Worked out? For whom? Certainly not her. She almost laughed, but couldn't quite do it.

He walked toward her, a new zip tie clasped

in his right hand, the gun held in his left. She curled her fingers around the handle of the knife.

He held the looped piece of plastic out to her. "You know how this works."

Isabelle raised her eyes and locked them on his. She whipped her hand out from beneath her thigh and buried the blade into the side of his.

His scream echoing in her ears, she launched herself to her feet and out the door.

TWENTY-ONE

They were two minutes out and Mac's nerves were stretched to the breaking point. In spite of trying to speed their way up the mountain, the twists and sharp curves had slowed them down way too much for Mac's comfort. *Hang on, Isabelle, please, hang on. Please, God, keep her alive. Don't let him hurt her.*

"Almost there," Creed said.

Yes, they were. After what seemed like an eternity, but in reality was only about twenty-two minutes, Creed braked.

"Don't miss it," Mac said. "According to the GPS, it's just ahead on the right."

"I know. I've patrolled the area before."

Of course he had. Mac snapped his lips shut and let out a low breath when Creed found the almost hidden drive and whipped the SUV into the opening. Creed pressed the gas and Mac glanced in the rearview mirror, noting the cars following.

When Creed stopped and shut off his lights, Mac knew exactly what the man was thinking. "Element of surprise?"

"Sure can't hurt. I'm just praying it's the right place." Mac didn't even want to think it wasn't. Creed radioed the others and they all flipped off their lights. Darkness pressed in, and right now, it was comforting, affording them the cover of the black night with only a sliver of moonlight to help guide them.

He pulled his weapon and climbed out of the cruiser. The four of them huddled together and Creed said, "Fan out. Grant, you head for the back of the house. Mac and I'll take the front. Ben, I know you're going to hate me, but I need you to hang here with the vehicles. If he tries to escape, this is probably the way he'll come."

"I've got it covered." Mac could tell he didn't like it but trusted him enough at this point to know if Travis came this way, he'd stop him.

Creed took the lead and Mac fell into step beside him. As they crested the slope in the drive, Mac saw the porch light burning as well as a light in the kitchen. Someone was there—unless the lights were on a timer and came on at a certain time after dark. *Please, God, let her be here.* Then he caught sight of the truck parked to the right of the cabin.

"That's Travis's," Creed said. "We've got the right place."

Relief and impatience swept over Mac. He just wanted to get in there and get Isabelle somewhere safe.

He pictured the simple ranch floor plan in his head. The porch steps led to a small foyer with a kitchen to the left, den straight ahead and all three bedrooms to the left.

On quiet feet, they approached.

Mac laid a hand on the Creed's shoulder. "Front door is open." It was cracked a fraction, so it would be easy to miss just glancing at the cabin, but—

"And that's blood," Creed said, pointing at the wet stains on the steps.

Mac's heart dropped. Creed walked to the front door and stepped to the side. He looked at Mac and Mac raised his weapon. All of his training rushed back along with the adrenaline of going after a criminal.

Creed used two fingers to push the wooden door open. Mac crouched and whipped inside toward the kitchen, his weapon ready. "Clear," he said softly, but loud enough for Creed to hear. Then back toward the den. He had a clear sight line of the entire room. "Clear," he said again.

"Hallway's clear," Creed said.

Mac followed him to clear the bedrooms. His

heart in his shoes, he drew in a deep breath. "She's not here."

"Yeah."

"And there's blood in the kitchen by the table in addition to the blood on the porch."

"I saw." Creed walked to the table, careful to skirt the blood spatter. "This is a contract for the sale of Isabelle's property. And it's signed."

Mac's blood ran cold. "He forced her to sign and now he's going to kill her. I'm searching the woods."

"Follow the blood trail. I'm right behind you."

Isabelle huddled behind the largest tree she could find, her breaths coming in short gasps that she tried to muffle. With her back against the trunk, she closed her eyes and listened. Her thundering heart impeded her efforts somewhat, but she held still, fingers clenched.

Footsteps crunched too close, and her eyes popped open. Moonlight filtered through the trees, but barely. Most of the undergrowth was dark, with only an occasional sliver of light slashing through the leaves above.

She prayed the darkness would work in her favor.

More crunching sounded as his footsteps drew near. *Footsteps* was a generous term. She could hear the limp and wondered that he could even walk at all. It must have been a flesh wound. She probably should have aimed for his stomach, but she'd chosen the target she could most easily get to. It had done what she'd intended and allowed her the time to run.

A flash of light caught her eye. Either he was using a flashlight or his phone to light his way. Desperate, she tried to think if she could have possibly left a trail.

She stayed still, the blood and adrenaline rushing through her veins. She wanted to move. To run and keep going until she found safety, but she was afraid he'd shoot her in the back. And she knew full well that he was an excellent marksman.

"Travis Lovett! We know you're out there! It's Creed, man. Turn yourself in and things will go better for you."

The footsteps stopped and Isabelle nearly went to her knees in relief. Creed had found her.

"Isabelle!"

And Mac. He'd come back.

For some reason that didn't surprise her. She knew that as soon as he'd heard she was missing, he would have been looking for her. Knew it like she knew her own name. As much as she wanted to rush from her hiding place, she continued to stay put, listening.

"Travis, come on, man," Creed called, "it's

over. We know you want Isabelle's land and are trying to force her to sell it. We found the documents in the kitchen."

A whispered curse just a few feet to her right froze her. He was to her right. Did she dare move? Try to head for the tree line? No doubt he'd hear her, but with the wound in his leg, she was fairly confident she could outrun him.

And as long as she stayed in the darker areas, she wouldn't give him a target.

"Isabelle? Can you answer me? Please?"

The hitch in Mac's voice nearly broke her heart. And made her decision. She darted out from behind the tree and raced in the direction of the voices, dodging limbs and leaves and trying not to trip on the underbrush. "Isabelle!" Travis's outraged cry spurred her on.

"Mac!"

"Isabelle!" Mac's joyous cry reached her.

A hand in her hair yanked her to a painful stop. She stumbled, bounced off a tree and went to the ground with a thud. Desperation swamped her. She rolled in spite of the grip on her hair and came face-to-face with Travis.

"Well," he ground out, "I guess you get to live a little longer."

Meaning, he planned to use her as a hostage to get out of the situation.

Not if she had anything to say about it.

A light landed on them and she blinked at the sudden brightness. "Let her go, Travis," Mac said, walking toward them with his weapon drawn and held on the man pinning her to the wooded floor.

Travis kept his grip in her hair with one hand and the gun at her temple with the other. Isabelle panted, drawing in a lungful of air, her gaze finally locking on Mac's.

The full-blown fury in his gaze said neither he—nor she—was going down without a fight. He held up a hand. "Travis, please, it's over. Let her go."

"Right. Like that's happening. I'm getting out of here. As long as you back up and let me get to my truck, I'll let her out a few miles from here. You know who I am now. I have no reason to kill her."

Except the tension running through him, the absolute rage that caused him to tremble, said he might just do it out of spite.

Isabelle didn't plan on finding out.

"Go," Travis said, pulling her to her feed and nudging her. "To the truck."

"We've already disabled your vehicle," Creed said. "It won't go anywhere."

"Then you'd better find me one that works. Because if I'm going down, she's going with me. I'll kill her right here while you watch. And I know you both well enough to know you don't want that to happen."

Isabelle continued to keep her eyes on Mac's. He lowered his gaze to the ground, then back up. To the ground, then back up.

She dropped. Travis screamed.

Gunfire exploded around her.

Travis hit the ground beside her, clutching his shoulder. A wound in his thigh bled freely. He still clutched his weapon and she flung a hand out to knock it out of Travis' reach.

"Isabelle! Move!"

Creed's shout spurred her to roll closer to Travis and press her hands against the wound in his thigh as it looked to be the most serious. "Don't kill him!"

Travis wasn't going to be hurting anyone at this point, anyway. He lay gasping, eyes wide with shock.

Creed and Grant raced to the man while Mac hurried toward her. Sirens screamed in the distance and vaguely, she realized they must have had an ambulance on standby.

"I'm sorry, Isabelle," Travis whispered.

"I am, too, Travis."

She stared, grief ripping through her at the betrayal of the friend she'd known and loved. So much to grieve. But sheer happiness erupted on the heels of the grief.

She was alive. And Mac was here.

When the paramedics dropped beside her, she moved back, hands held in front of her. Someone—Mac—poured water over them and she let him clean the blood from them. Then, strong arms wrapped around her and pulled her to her feet. She buried her face against Mac's shoulder and let the tears flow.

She wasn't sure how long she stood there with him holding her, but she finally managed to get herself under control and looked up at him. "You came back," she whispered. "I knew you would."

This time when he kissed her, there was no hesitation, no holding back. Isabelle once again lost track of time as she kissed him back, her heart overflowing with relief, gratitude and love. Yes, she loved him and knew that he loved her, too. She was confident that one day soon, he'd be ready to tell her exactly that. When he lifted his head, tears shimmered in his eyes. "I thought I'd lost you," he croaked.

"I know. I thought that this was it and I prayed. I prayed for you to find me, but if it wasn't to be, then I prayed for you to find peace. And healing."

He hugged her, squeezing the breath from her. She relished the feeling. When he released her, he stepped back. "I'm an idiot, Isabelle. I don't want to leave. I don't want to live in a big old house by myself on a ranch where there's no you or Katie or the others. I want to come back."

"Then come back. We'll even throw a party to celebrate your return."

He swallowed hard. "Just like that?"

"Just like that."

He hugged her once more. "I love you, Isabelle."

Tenderness filled her. "I know, Mac."

"Okay, then," he said, clasping her hand and tucking her under his arm. "Let's go home."

TWENTY-TWO

Three months later

Isabelle stood on the front porch and watched the children playing with the soccer ball in the clearing near the barn. The older boys tapped it back and forth between them, keeping it from Katie and from Lilly, who'd just figured out how to walk last week.

Katie let out a squeal and darted for the ball. She snagged it and ran toward the goal.

"Hey, squirt," Danny called, "that's cheating!"

Katie stood in the middle of the goal and jumped up and down. "I win! I win!" She threw the ball in the air and Milo, the Lab, went after it. He nosed it away from Katie and rolled it toward the barn. Sugar wasn't too far behind him.

The kids squealed, and Cody Ray, who stood at the door, shook his head, disappeared for a moment, then came back with another ball. He tossed it to Zeb, who used his head to pass it to Danny.

All the while she kept her eyes on the kids, she watched the drive. Mac had left over two hours ago to make a run into town and when she'd asked him where he was going, he'd given her a secretive smile and said, "I ordered something and just got a text that it was in. I'll be back soon."

She'd handed him a basket of Ms. Sybil's rolls. "Well, take these to Valerie, then, will you?"

"Of course."

Valerie had been cleared of any wrongdoing and was now working to recover from the consequences of her husband's actions. But she had a support system and she'd be all right in time.

Creed had asked Mac to join the force as one of the deputies and he'd agreed. He wore the Timber Creek Sheriff's Department uniform well and she could tell he was content with the decision. Frankly, so was she.

Finally, she spotted his truck and her heart thudded a faster rhythm like it always did when he was around. The last three months had been nothing short of amazing compared to the first couple of weeks she'd known Mac, and they'd spent many hours getting to know each other on an even deeper level. It was exhilarating to watch him come to life now that he'd decided to live.

He smiled more and took great joy in the kids. He also seemed to relish the fact that he could kiss her on a regular basis. Isabelle had to admit that was one of her favorite things, as well.

Along with the fact that one month, three weeks, four days ago, Cheryl had told her that Katie's mother had signed away her rights. The sassy little girl was up for adoption and Isabelle had immediately filled out the paperwork. She hadn't breathed a word of it to anyone except to Mac, and they prayed together every morning that God would see fit to allow Isabelle to adopt her.

Mac pulled to a stop and Isabelle frowned when she realized he wasn't alone. When the passenger door opened and a young woman stepped out, Isabelle sucked in a breath and ran to grab Lilly into her arms. She spun and hurried back to the driveway and, clutching the baby in one arm, threw the other around the girl. "Zoe!"

Zoe wrapped her arms around them both and squeezed. Lilly protested with a squeal and Zoe stepped back, a beautiful grin on her face. "Hey, Isabelle. I hope the surprise is okay. Mac said it would be."

"It's a wonderful surprise! I'm so glad to see you."

"I'm just here for a short visit, but I wanted you to see that I was clean now."

"I tried to come see you while you were in rehab."

"I know," Zoe said. She smiled. "They told me. That was one of the things that gave me the strength to keep fighting to beat the addiction."

Isabelle's throat clogged, but she managed a nod.

"Anyway," Zoe said, "My Aunt Fran in Texas wants me to come live with her while I finish school."

"I see."

Zoe's eyes went to the baby in Isabelle's arms. "She looks wonderful. Healthy and happy."

With grief and happiness mixing together, Isabelle passed the baby to her mother, praying Lilly wouldn't cry. After all, she didn't know her mother anymore. Isabelle cleared her throat. She'd known this day would come eventually, and now braced herself to say her goodbyes to the baby. "She's a joy. I'm going to miss her terribly." Lilly wrinkled her face and looked back at Isabelle, but she didn't cry.

Zoe pressed a kiss to the baby's forehead and handed her back to Isabelle. "I signed the papers today, giving you full custody." She pulled papers from her bag and handed them to Isabelle. "I also got Drew to give up his rights so you could keep Lilly and raise her as your own."

Isabelle's breath caught and a wave of dizziness hit her. "What?"

Zoe nodded. "I can't raise her—or love her—like you can. I decided the most *loving* thing I can do for her is to give her to you."

Isabelle passed Lilly to Mac this time, then wrapped the young girl in a hug. "I don't know what to say," Isabelle whispered.

"Say you'll love her and never let her forget that I love her, too."

"I promise." Isabelle hesitated. "Zoe, you're getting your life together. I can tell."

"I'm trying."

"I know you love Lilly. Why don't we do this. I'll keep her while you finish school. But know that you have a home here. A place to come back to. And a daughter to get to know."

Zoe cried on Isabelle's shoulder. Sobbed. Started to pull herself together then started all over again. She finally nodded. "I'd love that."

"Then that's the plan."

Zoe wiped her eyes and smiled. "Now I'm going to take a tour of the place and wrap myself in a few memories, then Cody Ray said he'd take me to the airport."

When she was out of earshot, Isabelle turned

to Mac and threw herself into the arm that wasn't holding Lilly. "Did that just happen?"

"Yep." He sounded almost as stunned as she felt.

"I get to keep her, Mac." She looked up and kissed him. When he let her go, she caught her breath, then looked him in the eye. "*We* get to keep her. And Katie, too."

Mac nodded. "Hey, Zeb! Come here a sec, will you?"

The boy jogged over and took Lilly from Mac, then darted back to the other kids.

"Mac? What are you doing?"

He dropped to one knee. "I don't want to wait any longer." He dug into his front pocket while Isabelle tried to breathe.

"Mac?"

"I know when I arrived, I had some major baggage, but you were right when you said being here was healing for me. While I'd come a long way in the healing process before I met you, it was being here with you and the kids and the others that completed it. When I thought I'd lost you that day to Travis Lovett, I nearly came unglued. The truth is, I knew that day I wanted to spend the rest of my life with you, living here, raising kids—ours and those who are in the system—for as long as we have them." He pulled his hand out of his pocket and a sparkling diamond rested in his palm. "It's small, but it was bought with all my love. I love you, Isabelle. Will you marry me?"

She nodded. "Yeah, Mac, I'll marry you."

"She said yes!"

His shout carried across to the kids playing. They stopped and whooped and ran to embrace her and Mac just as another car pulled into the drive.

Cheryl got out and had a big smile on her face. "You got the boys, too!"

Her announcement set off more shouting and hollers and tears and hugs. "Hey," Zeb said, "this calls for a celebration. I think we need s'mores on the new firepit."

Finally, after everyone calmed down and had their fill of s'mores, Cody Ray packed Zoe into his truck and they headed to the airport. Cheryl waved her goodbyes while munching on a s'more.

Isabelle stood on the porch waving back, her heart so full she wasn't sure it wouldn't rupture. *Thank you, God, for...everything.*

Mac stepped up beside her and pulled her to him one more time. "Thank you for not giving up on me."

"And thank you for applying to be my handyman."

He grinned, then sobered. "The future is

going to have ups and downs, but as long as we're side by side, we'll come through it better people. I truly believe the best is yet to come, Isabelle."

"And we'll jump into it with both feet. Together."

"Together."

With that, he took her hand and they walked to the firepit to spoil their dinner with s'mores and their children with love.

* * * * *

If you enjoyed this story, look for these other Love Inspired Suspense books by Lynette Eason:

Holiday Homecoming Secrets
Holiday Amnesia
Vanished in the Night

Dear Reader,

I hope the end of this story finds you smiling. I wrote this story in the middle of the 2020 pandemic, and I'll admit, I needed to write something that made me smile. While I fell in love with my characters Mac and Isabelle, I have to say that every time little Katie stepped onto the page, she made me grin. And that was a good thing. I'm blessed to have a Katie in my life. Her name is Shelby and she's my six-year-old niece. I hope during these unusual times you have a Katie in your life. Not necessarily a five-year-old, but someone who's there to make you smile or chuckle at least once or twice a day. If you don't, then know I'm praying God sends you someone. In the meantime, I'm so honored that you picked up this book and I pray that it blessed you in some way. If you'd like to stay in touch, my website is www.lynetteeason.com and you can find me on Facebook at www.Facebook.com/lynette.eason. I'm on Twitter, @lynetteeason, and Instagram, @lynetteeason. Happy reading to all!

Much love,
Lynette

Get 4 FREE REWARDS!

We'll send you 2 FREE Books plus 2 FREE Mystery Gifts.

Her Hometown Detective
Elizabeth Mowers

Bride on the Run
Anna J. Stewart

Harlequin Heartwarming Larger-Print books will connect you to uplifting stories where the bonds of friendship, family and community unite.

FREE
Value Over
$20

YES! Please send me 2 FREE Harlequin Heartwarming Larger-Print novels and my 2 FREE mystery gifts (gifts worth about $10 retail). After receiving them, if I don't wish to receive any more books, I can return the shipping statement marked "cancel." If I don't cancel, I will receive 4 brand-new larger-print novels every month and be billed just $5.74 per book in the U.S. or $6.24 per book in Canada. That's a savings of at least 21% off the cover price. It's quite a bargain! Shipping and handling is just 50¢ per book in the U.S. and $1.25 per book in Canada.* I understand that accepting the 2 free books and gifts places me under no obligation to buy anything. I can always return a shipment and cancel at any time. The free books and gifts are mine to keep no matter what I decide.

161/361 HDN GNPZ

Name (please print)

Address   Apt. #

City   State/Province   Zip/Postal Code

Email: Please check this box ☐ if you would like to receive newsletters and promotional emails from Harlequin Enterprises ULC and its affiliates. You can unsubscribe anytime.

Mail to the **Harlequin Reader Service:**
IN U.S.A.: P.O. Box 1341, Buffalo, NY 14240-8531
IN CANADA: P.O. Box 603, Fort Erie, Ontario L2A 5X3

Want to try 2 free books from another series? Call 1-800-873-8635 or visit www.ReaderService.com.
